MW01223881

The
Molotov
Cocktail

Prize Winners
Anthology

Vol. 5

Edited by Josh Goller

Editor: Josh Goller
Associate Editor: Mary Lenoir Bond

ISBN: 979-8-6722-1376-7

Contents

Legends:

Wild:

The Molotov Cocktail

MONSTERS

"Monsters are the patron saints
of imperfection."
– Guillermo del Toro

The Molotov Cocktail

Ursa Major

By Jen Corrigan

We are eight years old when our father begins to change.

After the first doctor's appointment, we sit on his lap in the big chair, a sister to each knee. He shows us the coarse hair sprouting from his forearms. We run our palms over the bristly patches, and he jokes about his right to *bear* arms. Lifting his shoulders, he flexes, one arm over, one under, like a glistening bodybuilder posing on stage.

When we don't want to go to bed, our father chases us around the house, growling and snarling, gnashing his teeth in jest. He catches us in his hands, more paw-like each day, and lifts us to his mouth as if to eat us. Our mother stands against the wall, hugging her chest.

At breakfast, our father lets us take bites of his cereal, calling us both Goldilocks, even though our hair is short and muddy brown. I bring the spoon to my mouth and declare his plain Cheerios too hot, my sister echoing too cold. Our father grabs our faces and kisses our foreheads roughly, proclaiming we are just right. We pull away, red marks where our father's fangs have pierced the skin.

In the winter evenings, we lie on the floor and snuggle into our father's sides. He watches survival shows on TV while my sister and I watch the flicker of snow against the window pane. His chest has grown outward, his shoulders muscled and knotty. We run our fingertips along the curved blades pushing from under his nails although our mother tells us not to. Our father lies belly-down against the floor, arms out, eyes glassy and mouth open. When I'm old and gone, he jokes, you can turn me into a rug and keep me forever! When we are shooed off to bed, I turn in the hallway and peer around the corner, watch my father pull my mother down onto him in an embrace I am not meant to see.

After the last doctor's appointment, our father is solemn and withdrawn. When he snaps his jaws at my sister for the first and only time, our mother banishes him to the bedroom. She brings him his meat, increasingly rare, three times a day, then four, five. We are not allowed inside. When our mother goes to sleep in the guest bedroom, we creep down the hallway and sit on the floor outside our father's room. We press our ears against the door and listen to the growls reverberating through the wood.

Our father becomes unruly, impossible, when winter breaks into spring. He stops speaking, communicates with roars. When he knocks our mother to the ground, she knows it's time. It's for the best, she tells us, her eyes wet and red.

She makes us stay in our bedroom that night. He wouldn't want you to see him like this, she tells us, but we watch through the upstairs window anyway. We listen to the snap of our mother throwing open the bedroom door, then the front door, hollering to startle our father out. The house shakes as his heft gallops, slowly at first, then faster. It is a dark night, but clear, the stars bright as fire. We watch our father's body move over the grass, the dew shimmering in his fur. I grab my sister's hand and bring it up to the window. We point together at the sky, tracing the handle of the Big Dipper, the only constellation we ever learned.

#

Jen Corrigan is a prose writer who lives in Iowa. Recently, her work has appeared in *Catapult, Literary Hub, Gay Magazine*, and *Salon*. Visit her at www.jen-corrigan.com.

The Lamppost Huggers

By Christopher Stanley

It's six-thirty on a slush-wet Wednesday morning and I'm the only person at the bus stop who isn't nervous. Other commuters stare, mouths open, absent-mindedly scratching the backs of their wrists. On the far side of the road, an old man hugs a lamppost. In the orange light, his skin is sallow and wrinkled, his hair silver and flecked with snow. He's naked apart from a pair of threadbare pyjama shorts, and when he moves, his belly peels away from the frozen metal like Velcro.

It isn't just the old man who makes the other commuters nervous, it's what he represents. We've all seen the pictures in the news. We've heard the stories of ordinary people leaving their homes in the dead of night, with no clothes or shoes, searching for a lamppost to hug. They don't speak and won't let go without becoming hostile or suicidal. The best anyone can do is to keep them warm so they don't die from exposure. Yes, we've seen the photos, but that was London, Birmingham, Manchester. Not here. Not in our neighbourhood.

Not until this morning.

Two days later, the old man is gone. In his place is a younger woman with a dressing gown tied loosely around her waist. There's something intimate about the way she hugs the lamppost, her ear pressed to its metal skin, a contented smile playing on her lips. Her husband is slumped on a nearby bench while her children tug on her dressing gown.

The woman isn't the only lamppost hugger on the high street this morning. Her family aren't the only ones mourning the loss of someone who's still alive. For as far as I can see in both directions, people of all ages cling to lampposts like lovers during a last dance.

The government has declared a state of national emergency, but the huggers don't respond to curfews. Phrases like 'mass hysteria' and 'viral epidemic' have flown into the headlines and nested there. A video emerged of a priest in Rotherham persuading a lamppost-hugging member of his congregation to let go. For a day or so, the country dared to hope. Then the priest was photographed in red paisley pyjamas, engaging in his own unorthodox embrace.

According to the leaflets, we're supposed to sleep with our clothes on. Not just clothes, but winter coats and boots. On the way home from work, I tell the bus driver this is no way to live. What's happening right now is a test of our national character and the only way to beat it is through strength of mind. That's why I still sleep in a T-shirt and shorts. That's why I'm still here and my neighbours are gone.

"I preferred it when the high street was lined with trees," says the bus driver as I step onto the icy pavement. "The birds did, too."

At home, I lie in bed and listen to the anguished howls of families begging their loved ones to come inside. I tell myself it won't be me. Not tonight. I repeat this over and over until it's imprinted on my subconscious.

I don't know what time it is when the high-pitched squeal

tears me from my dreams. I clamp my hands over my ears and bury my head under the pillow, but the sound just gets louder, ringing like unchecked feedback from a guitar amp. Nauseous and disorientated, I fight my way out of bed and bump through the darkness, certain the noise must be coming from outside. On the way downstairs, I cling to the banister and vomit on the carpet. Then I unlock the front door and fall face-first into the snow.

It isn't really me who grabs the lamppost. By the time I reach the far side of the road, I've lost the capacity for rational thought. The way a tortured man will confess to crimes he didn't commit, I'm willing to try anything. The moment my skin touches the metal, the noise changes, the lamppost acting like some kind of antenna. Gone is the screaming static. Instead, my head is filled with the soothing music of angels. Beautiful overlapping melodies. Notes as delicate as the falling snow.

This must be what heaven sounds like.

Then I hear another noise above me. A low, soft *whoomph*. I look up into the darkness, waiting and wondering. The smell arrives first, ripe and sticky like the local dump. Then the creature lands on the arm of the lamppost, each wing as wide as a bus. Its toes are mattress springs and vacuum cleaner hoses, curled into lawnmower-blade talons. Its feathers are shredded pillow cases and ironing-board covers. The way it jerks and twitches, it reminds me of birds on a feeder. But there aren't any birds this big. And this one has three heads, massive like chimineas, with dangerously hooked beaks.

The creature is the source of the song I can hear. I don't care if it's an angel calling me to heaven or a siren luring me to my demise; I'm ready either way. The middle head stops singing and twists to one side, inspecting me with a black webcam eye. I reach up and it lunges towards me, hissing and spitting, its beak stretched impossibly wide. One snap of those fearsome jaws and my head would come clean off. And maybe I should be afraid, but I'm not. I'm its servant, its disciple, and as long as it sings to me it may do whatever it desires. But something else snatches its attention.

The night bus, growling like a beast up the high street.

The middle head twists towards the others, hissing instructions, and with a flap of its wings, the creature disappears over the rooftops. I panic and start to follow, but the moment I let go of the lamppost, the noise returns. I'm winded by the cold. I fall back and press my ear to the soothing metal.

It's okay. I can still hear its song.

#

Christopher Stanley lives on a hill in England with three sons who share a birthday but aren't triplets. He is the author of numerous prize-winning flash fictions, the darkest of which can be disturbing the peace in his debut collection, *The Lamppost Huggers and Other Wretched Tales*, published by *The Arcanist* in June 2020.

Our Immortal Night

By Neil Clark

A time ago, my wife and I befriended an immortal in the pub.

We all hit it off so well that we invited him back to ours after closing time. A line or six of the old Bolivian marching powder later, the guy was telling us everything. From what sword he used to slay the Auld Enemy on the battlefields of Bannockburn, to the way he enjoyed the stench of people's infected limbs at the height of the bubonic plague.

He got all emotional after that. Said it gets lonely, being an immortal. Knowing everyone you meet is going to be rotting in the ground within the relative blink of an eye.

He explained how he'd come to look at time. How he approached the whole concept like a mortal would approach doing lengths of a swimming pool. Each generation is like a length, he said. It hurts at first, and the thought of taking a deep breath and starting another seems impossible. But you must push through that. Eventually, although the pain never eases, you put it to the back of your mind and just keep swimming. It's the only way, he said. Or else you'll drown. And drowning is quite the unpleasant prospect for an immortal.

There wasn't a dry eye in the house. We had a big group hug and my wife told him that, even though we might not be exactly the same as him, we know how he feels. Life, she said, whatever that word means in the context of our conversation, is simply a bitch. It whimpers on and suffers and can never be put down even when there's a vet saying it really should be.

I wanted to contribute something to the conversation, so I told him I'd seen the film *Highlander* when it was in cinemas and thought it was quite good.

Then, at six in the morning, he went out for some fresh air, and my wife and I just thought, 'Ah fuck it. When he comes back, let's tie him up and never let him go for eternity. See what happens.'

By the time we got the duct tape to hold him in place up in the rafters of our living room, sunlight was starting to pour in, making everything all balmy and suffocating.

Our night was at a crossroads. We could turn left: go for a nice lie-down, put a lid on it and sleep through the day as usual. Or, we could turn right: get the party started again.

We shut the curtains and took a hard right. Got a delivery in off Abraham, our supplier from the hospital, and within seconds of resuscitation, our attentions were focused on how we could have some serious fun with our immortal friend.

The bleach was my wife's idea. Boil it with some paracetamol and pump it down his throat, she suggested. See what it's like to watch how he doesn't die.

After that, we slit his wrists and sipped on Bloody Marys, watching him writhe around up there with his airways all taped up, draining and disinfecting and suffocating away for a week or more.

We noticed he'd gone all quiet at some point during all the

shenanigans, so we started grilling him. First, with questions about being an immortal, and then, literally, using this George Foreman thing that Amazon erroneously sent us back in 2002.

On the topic of what it takes to kill an immortal, he confirmed to us that the only way to achieve it is by beheading.

But what is the cut-off point for beheading, as opposed to just dissecting?

We set about putting this to the test, starting from the waist up, using a sword from the Middle Ages we'd acquired.

Off went his legs, then his stomach. He was still breathing, even when his ribcage and lungs got the chop.

Indeed, after his legs, his bleached stomach and intestines, his livers, kidneys, lungs, heart and lean, mean, fat-free skin were sat in a pile, rotting away on the floor, he was still very much alive on the rafters. Just a pair of arms, collar bones, a neck and a head with blinking, lucid eyes.

Concerned that if we cut a centimeter higher, it might count as a beheading, we decided to stop and have a moment of reflection.

We recalled the metaphorical crossroads we came to that night so many months before, pondering what might have been had we simply taken a gentler turn to the left.

Perhaps we had gotten ourselves a little carried away. Maybe we had been trying to suppress some kind of monster inside us. Yet alas, in attempting to do so, we had ended up feeding whatever monster had reared its head on the outside, my wife suggested.

With nothing to add to that, I simply said that I had seen the controversial Metallica documentary *Some Kind of Monster* and remembered finding it quite interesting.

Let's put a lid on it, we agreed. And when we wake, it's a quiet night down the pub and no more. One Bloody Mary apiece, then home to Rafter Boy, who we were kind of stuck with now, given his recently acquired mobility issues.

But hey, we agreed. Let us have no regrets.

For life, in the context of this conversation, is endless and vapid. And these are the lengths to which we sometimes must go to cut through the grave times, to ensure we do not drown in this interminable pool of turgid mundanity, said my wife.

I nodded and suggested we watch something on Netflix before turning in.

#

Neil Clark still uses his old George Foreman grill from 2002, but not in that way. Find him on Twitter @NeilRClark or visit neilclarkwrites.wordpress.com.

Indoors

By Travis Dahlke

The first place I truly realized that I was being followed by mildew was the third home my family had in Hennequin, Texas. Before, there was the carpet of my childhood bedroom, spongy and sour to bare feet. Then, the blackening shower curtain at my uncle's timeshare in St. Barts that seemed to sicken like a frostbite victim. A summer away from home at 4-H camp where, as we slept, splotches came exploring from the ceiling corners. Fuzz aimed right at my bunk. The counselors fired bleach, which only came back to stain their clothes pink.

'It's the darnedest thing,' was all anyone could say.

People claimed the land under the house in Hennequin was cursed out with spirits because a mass shooter grew up there. But it was said also by my Grandpa Higby (who studied at Yale) that rotten walls could make people hallucinate—though how could we all be hallucinating the same thing?

Then Grandpa Higby moved in with us because he couldn't remember anything, and all day he sat in his chair laughing at soaps. The sad ones. His sickness accelerated at an impossible pace, and he turned black just like that shower curtain.

The hospital told us Higby succumbed to lethal levels of airborne toxins in our home. We left it to the next family.

It found me in the half-finished basement of Harris Benjamin's house. During seven minutes in heaven, where on the other side of the Sprite bottle threads was Gabby Bernstein from Pre-Calc in her Iron Maiden shirt and invisible braces. We were put in the linen closet where Harris's family hid things they didn't want to think about anymore. '(You Make Me Feel Like) A Natural Woman' came deadened from a boombox outside the door. Gabby's bra stuffing crumpled against me, our gums forming a nervous cinnamon humidity. Then, the taste of pennies.

Gabby, who was allergic to cut grass, ran screaming from the closet, spouts of blood running from her eyes and nose. In the dark next to Battleship and Mr. Benjamin's scummy old *Playboy*s, the spores whispered:

Good. She's gone.

They branded me 'Davey the Antichrist.' Two schools and one dorm were torn down. Our town's Burger Palace, where I worked drive-thru, was condemned by the health inspector. Bryn Capitol, where I interned, was shuttered up. The insurance company where I nearly made partner turned to slime, capped by a state-of-the-art HVAC system for a building I knew had always been marked for death. All diagnosed with 'irremediable blooms of penicillium breeding with asbestos.'

Alone in my apartment, every power-strip loaded with dehumidifiers, it said:

We don't want them anyway. You don't need money.

Was it when I tore all the moss from that albino boulder or when I knocked over that abandoned shack in the woods with triangles drawn on its walls? Did my parents make some bargain over their firstborn? I considered escaping my hex for good, but that'd be giving it what it wants. Inheritance.

Don't leave us yet, David.

I met Suzanne on the way to CVS to buy the Sprite I'd pair with triple the Benadryl. She had been burned by yellow jackets and needed a spare EpiPen. She was missing a tooth, which made her whistle. We were married inside a year.

Our son, Douglas, was named after a fake president from a movie. We agreed on raising him in Utah, the second driest state in which to live. You could leave a bag of chips out in the open and they'd never go stale. The neighborhood came pre-made out of a box, with terracotta shingles that would fade gradually at the same rate as us.

It was Christmas when the murders started. First was Maura Studebaker, at the 'cul' of our cul-de-sac. It was a reminder that skin was only temporary and we'd crumple if not for having to protect our own children from the knowledge of this. The attacker descended from her wine attic, and using a handheld, box vegetable/cheese grater, she chaffed Maura Studebaker's face to the skull. Earlier it had been wrapped under her tree (the grater, not her face). A curfew was instated. We cemented the doors.

Douglas was terrified to be alone. He'd plead with us to stay outside or sleep at friends' houses.

'There are noises in the wall,' he'd say. 'At night when it's quiet, I can hear laughter. From the floor.'

'You're too old for monsters in floors. We're safe here.'

Suzanne took it badly. I could smell she was smoking again and trying to hide it. We had to wash Douglas's bedding once a week. I found our electric whisker in his room. The shingles lost all charm.

It came back. First, as veins from the basement, and then, by storm clouds soaking above our heads. A swamp carpet. Radiator belching out what rot cooked behind the walls. I'd dial the thermostat down, only to find it turned back up in the morning. The neighborhood went dormant. Waiting. We lived coughing in a prison of urine and tobacco. Suzanne's keys went missing.

'You leave them out of this, you fuck.'

Silence.

I came home from work early to a Good-Guys Remediation truck in our driveway. Rushing his estimate so he could get out before dark.

'This is going to cost you,' he said, motioning to the leafy, black hair. 'See the saturation here?' A wolverine's back. We couldn't stop prying. Digging into the floor. Fingering living mud. When the drywall was pulled away, we saw it.

A body. Swaddled in green velvet.

The remediator didn't put down his knife until we were safe on the lawn, away from the liberated bog.

They found Maura's earrings in what had been the man's nest. Suzanne's keys. The coroner report noted it was death by rapid fungal asphyxiation.

The air lost all sharpness. A wasp parting with its stinger. A little kind of goodbye.

#

Travis Dahlke is a writer from Connecticut with work forthcoming or appearing in *Joyland Magazine, Outlook Springs, SAND Journal, Structo,* and *The Longleaf Review,* among other literary journals and collections. Find his work at deffbridges.com.

I've Seen the Other Shadow in the City

By Emma Miller

Lately, I've been catching glimpses of myself. I don't mean in storefront windows.

I've taken to long walks in the city. Down empty streets and under highways, through alleyways and marketplaces, sometimes even over the long northern bridge, just to turn around when I reach the end of it. I like the invisibility of it, the slipping between. I see everything. The flower market pickpockets, the paper district price-gougers, the place where the butcher dumps blood in the river, late, when he thinks no one is watching.

When I do sleep, it's in the kinds of places you pay for by the hour. Back rooms in dives, back rows of buses. It's rainy this time of year, all fog and shadow, and I rarely take the same route twice.

I think that's why it took so long for me to notice her.

The first time, I thought it was a trick of the darkness. A trolley passed by, and in its window, I saw her face.

A few days later, I saw her again, illuminated by the sallow light of a streetlamp, a reflection in wax.

The next morning I asked for coffee, and the deli man said he'd just given me one. When I went outside, I saw myself sitting on a bench across the street, drinking coffee.

Now I see her everywhere.

It's little things: a familiar coat in a crowd, a boot disappearing around a corner, the uncanny feeling of seeing the back of your own head. The questions seep under my skin with the city fog. I wonder whether she wants something. Whether she'll do anything for it. Whether my hair is really as thin as hers seems to be; whether my teeth are really as pointed.

What you must know is that these things have rules. Garlic and crosses, silver and pentagrams. Even if you and I don't understand them, there are always rules.

One of hers, which I discovered after several weeks, is that I determine her routes. She appears in the places that I was precisely 24 hours before. Following me, and always arriving a day late.

I was, if not content, resigned to watching her from this distance. Until the day she reached for me.

I had just boarded a trolley. I turned around, and her hand was inches from my face. The door snapped shut just before she could reach it, and for a terrible moment, her fingertips lingered on the glass. Only when we pulled away did I remember the car I'd missed the day before.

But I hadn't left my hand on the trolley for so long. I hadn't gazed after it so intently.

And most importantly, I hadn't *seen* anyone. Not like she had so clearly, for the first time, seen me.

That night, I stand before the mirror, naked. I touch the features of my face until it frightens me and I must turn out the light.

What you must know is that there is a place near the northern bridge where the trolley tracks turn sharply, enough that the conductor cannot see around the bend. There is an old signal box there, with five steps and one door and one window, but the signal is broken and the box unmanned. The trolley passes this signal at 3:40 p.m. It does not run on weekends.

I arrive at this place on Sunday afternoon, and it is raining so hard I have to duck inside to light my cigarette. At 3:39, I step forward and—fighting a sharp jab of fear, even though I know the trolley is not coming today—I lay my body across the tracks.

The rain falls on my unprotected face, and I am a cadaver in a battlefield.

I wait. Five minutes. Ten. Thirty. Then, soaked and shaking, I stand. That should be enough time, even if the trolley is delayed.

On Monday morning, it has stopped raining, but I wake up with a bad cold, head hazy and throat cracked and lungs full of yellow. I go to the signal box early, coughing between cigarettes. When the moment comes, I stand to look out the window.

There is a heavy footfall on the steps outside.

Damn it all to hell.

Thump.

Before I laid down on the tracks yesterday.

Thump.

I lit my cigarette in the signal box.

Thump.

What you must know is that the signal box is five steep stairs, one door, and one window.

Thump.

More essential is that it is five stairs that have creaked under five footfalls. One door whose handle is turning. And one window that I am now realizing is impossibly tight to scramble through, even as I suck in my stomach, even as I wish myself small, even as I claw at the decaying wood, driving splinters under my nails.

A cold, familiar hand wraps around my ankle.

I kick, foot hitting air. The hand pulls and I pull back. Another yank, another flurry of struggle. I scream. I kick. And I push, *push*, will myself through the window. My chest is through. My torso is through. My hip pops, wrenches out of its socket — I scream again — and then my legs are through, and I'm tumbling down the side of the box, sprawling on the tracks below.

Crumpled, I gaze up at my face in the signal house window. Watching myself watching myself watching myself watching myself.

And in the window, she looks terrified. Terrified and relieved.

As I said before. The corner is so sharp, I do not see the trolley —

#

Emma Miller is a writer and editor in New York City, where she writes facts by day and fiction by night. Her work has appeared in *The Molotov Cocktail, Daily Science Fiction, Apparition Literary Magazine, Flash Fiction Magazine,* and other outlets.

Manticore

By Stuart Airey

The Emirati will own it, but I will build it. The first tower over one kilometre high, dwarfing even the Burj Khalifa. We are already at a height that satisfies emperors, the gulf shining from Doha to Suza.

I let the speed creep up on the desert road home, knowing Naia is waiting.

It is a blur on my right and I think it looks up at me before we hit. For a moment, we are one sickening thing. Then the road is empty again. I don't stop.

I shine my cell phone on the front of the car at home. The grill is torn and I pull fur from a crack in the bumper. It is fine and golden. There is nothing more. There is an exquisite newness in the taste of Naia that night. I am awake long after, listening to the rhythm of her sleep. My arthritic hip is painless.

I look, but there is no roadkill in the morning. It is a restless day of paperwork. At last, I am standing on the open steel frame, looking down at the glass wonder that is Dubai. I feel perfectly balanced.

I open my tongue to the moisture of altitude. I feel like I'm growing a tail.

I stop and look up at the stars on the way home. I hear ancient whispering patterns filling the night sky. It is a language much older than Arabic. I realise I've driven home without car lights. I am aware of small scuttling animals sharing the desert. I look in the bathroom mirror. My pupils are oval and pointed.

Naia screams as we make love. My spine is so flexible. She rises softly before dawn. I lie curled and still as she leaves. We have no voice for each other, though I think she has a word for what I am becoming. I have a terrible headache in the morning light.

The day is just tolerable in sunglasses. I spend it all in my office. I have a Kandura and Ghutrah brought up, it is time to hide my tail. I feel each porcupine quill budding and sharpening, probing the subtle air currents. I feel the poison sacs fill with a golden warmth. I have a burning need to hunt.

At last, I stand on the pure steel of the new shafts, and the night is velvet. I place my clawed fingers on the skeleton of the building. I can sense the building as a living thing, following its veins and arteries deep into the earth. Beneath the building is the rustling of ancient things, scarabs that undulate like music. They have waited an age for my call.

I run down the sides of the structure, the air fluid and buoyant, and my tail is joyous. Down and down I glide as the city sounds a thousand murmurs. As I reach the ground, I am for a moment impossibly and gloriously still. I feel the earth as a heaving swell on which the living mingle with the dead.

I read the rise and fall of empires as an unfurling scroll.

Dubai is a pious plum by day, a peeled and opened flesh by night. It suits me to be faceless. I seek the oldest and wealthiest nightlife first and take them in the shadows. They are wrinkled skins with the barest dry fruit. The young are an exquisite explosion.

The city is prostrate with prayer by day. Everyone is veiled in shared secrecy. The women gather by afternoon in shuttered apartments, lighting incense and speaking incantations over each other. The men fire their guns in the noon heat and find old alliances. There is an official lie that no one believes. Families check in hourly by Facebook.

I am becoming multiple. They are my scarabs now, reptilian and calm. We are a hibernation.

The city is a throbbing ache at the back of my throat. The desert sand stretches its phosphorescent skin under the building, curling and uncurling. I hold open the slit of an eye. Tonight, we will be a flood.

They come an hour before sunset. I am sleepily aware of the lift ascending. Naia and her sister. Veiled in formal Burqa, but they are as fluttering birds to me. I know all languages but not this one they are chanting. Their open hands are suppliant with a timeless grace. I know they wear amulets against their throats, passed down through the ages. I see a spidery web of lines shimmering in the air between us.

There is this moment when we are one. We are the shape of an egg, encrusted with forgotten stones. We are above the desert singing songs to each other. We are a rippling thing of feathers and scales. We are shellfish, we are moths. We are bearded, we are smooth. Our fingers are entwined.

We understand everything. That is when Naia plunges in the dagger.

#

Stuart Airey lives in Hamilton, New Zealand and wanders the labyrinths of his tortured mind, occasionally putting pen to paper. He was a finalist in the Sarah Broom Poetry Prize 2018 and has been published in the *Ocotillo Review*. He has performed several multimedia poetry evenings and is working on his breakthrough project.

Ink

By Alpheus Williams

I walk through customs and security checks, an old man with a walking stick. Safe as houses, safe as a bank, old, unarmed and harmless. The immigration officer kindly welcomes me home.

It's been a long time, sir.

Indeed it has.

I rent a car at the airport. Things have changed. Traffic runs bumper-to-bumper with a backdrop of mountains draped in smoke haze and smog. Millions of people live this every day. Too busy surviving the endgame to fix the now game. It's sad.

But it's okay. I'm here to help. I bring liberation and renewal. Cool, huh?

I drive to Carlsbad down the coast between L.A. and San Diego. It's a nice place, but it used to be nicer. The traffic has left me edgy.

I rent a unit close to the beach so I can walk along the promenade in the mornings and breathe the winds that travel the world.

There are so many crows. They squawk and cry out and fly in and out of the palm leaves high on the trunks overlooking the city and the beach. I like crows, survivors, but I miss the sweet notes of songbirds, larks and mockingbirds. They don't seem to be around anymore and I wonder how many have noticed. People walk their dogs on leads. I like dogs, but I wonder what happened to the coyotes and bobcats. The condors and brown bears have disappeared long ago, along with the wolves and the tule elk. People walk and jog along the road that borders the beach. Many have earbuds in their ears, wired into elsewhere.

It saddens me, along with the apartments and mobile homes and homeless squeezed in together to feel the breeze of a dying ocean. Destined to the fate of battery hens. Do they miss the birdsong as I do or are they content to plug their ears with wires and play make-believe?

The silver head of my walking stick burns through the palm of my hand. Folklore got it right. Silver and my kind don't mix. But pain teaches control and respect and I am no longer slave to the moon.

A man pulls up in a large, rumbling Hummer one morning as I walk along the promenade. Queries my limp. There's no room for an answer. He can't stop talking about his own leg, his drug abuse and being born a Catholic in a family of eight children, strayed from God, became addicted to drugs but was reborn and saved. Exchanging one addiction for another. He told me his whole boring life in the space of traffic light change. He looks at me as if we're brothers and quotes the ridiculous:

The Lord breaks the legs of those He wants to keep close to the fold.

He grins as if his withered limb is a blessing. He's in insurance, gives me his business card. Big mistake. I find him later as the moon fills the sky. I'm not a raving, thoughtless, compulsive killer. It's not about hunger or the moon. It's about other things.

He answers the doorbell. Looks puzzled, then recognises me. Big, shaky smile. I morph in front of him, sweep him into the foyer, eat his face, paint the walls with him, having a hell of time. His wife enters the room, screams. I try to get the words around my dripping fangs and lolling tongue, not to worry because it's Wednesday and I don't eat women on Wednesday. She doesn't appreciate the levity.

Her husband is dripping from the walls. It's been fun, I say, leaving her screaming and pulling her hair. Sorry. I can't help but laugh. I mean, really, the guy was an asshole. I tell her to get rid of the Hummer and buy something more environmentally responsible, an electric car or hybrid perhaps. Like her husband, she's too busy with her own shit to pay attention. These people, it's always about them. I shake my head. I can tarry no longer. I have serious business the following day.

It only takes a scratch and soupcon of the virus to become like me, and I have buckets of the stuff in my stock of tattoo inks. The best reds, whites, and blues money can buy, and I'm selling cheap.

I give my card to the distributor. He's shady and slimier than snot from a snail, but he covers every tattoo parlour on the Southern California coast accessing all the military bases, outlaw motorcycle clubs, drug cartel underlings, smitten lovers and other aficionados of body art.

I play an easy mark, feign outrage when he haggles my price, but I sell to him anyway. After all, it's not about the money, and I have buckets of the stuff.

Hell, I am the stuff.

I am liberation. Time to set free the hoards.

Semper fi!

Death before Dishonour!

Mom!

Winged skulls and love hearts!

De opresso liber!

I chuckle. Interesting times ahead. Man, things are really going to pop come the next full moon. I would love to stick around and watch, but I have loads more ink and a serious market opening in Asia. I must be gone.

Busy, busy, busy.

#

Alpheus Williams lives and writes in a tiny village tucked away along the coast of NSW, Australia. He spends a lot of time trying to explore and understand the unseen beauty of things.

Sawdust

By James Turner

The man slips the still chainsaw from the tree trunk. Amongst the sawdust and oily stains on his overalls, the label reads 'Billy.' He presses a hand to the elm tree, a slow crack echoes through the forest, and it descends to the bed of bracken.

Daylight falls across the clearing and the circle of tree stumps. Billy runs his cracked fingertips over their initials, her face hidden in the shadows of his mind. The smell of damp earth sweeps past on a slight breeze. Chunks of dark hair poke from Billy's hat and a beard creeps up his cheeks, towards grey eyes. The sun slips behind some clouds, and he drops his heavy frame to the warm rings of the stump. Her laughter floats through the undergrowth, hiding behind trees and under bushes. Billy looks down at his hands, no longer young and sticky with sap, and closes his eyes.

The chainsaw roars to life, slicing off a five-foot log, which Billy drags up to the cabin. He lifts it onto his workbench and switches on the kettle. The wall covered with woodworking tools, each cleaned and oiled and back on their hook. He works one end of the elm into a dome, the amber rings stretched over exposed grain, and with a chisel, he shapes a mouth. Blowing away the sawdust, the lips part and take a deep breath.

'Finally,' they say, revealing a straight set of wooden teeth. 'I've been trapped in this elm for forty-three years. Please give me a pair of eyes so I can see.'

Billy's head drops, and he pours himself another coffee. He gouges out the indents of two eyes, soft and youthful, and they blink open.

'There you are,' the mouth says, eyes moving around the room. 'Thank you. Could you whittle me up some ears next?'

The man works through the night, hands blistered and moustache stained with coffee. A face appears. A pinched nose, high cheekbones, full lips and waves of cropped hair. It is the face of the man's first wife, the face that follows him through the trees.

'They used to hang people from those elms,' the mouth says, eyes on the cabin door. 'I watched them all die. Are they still out there?'

'Most are gone,' Billy says, sharpening his file, as he shapes the crevices of an ear. 'I'm trying to find my wife, Hazel. She died out there too.'

'What did you do to the others?'

The first was by accident, a desperation to keep Hazel real until the mouth came to life. It screamed until he drilled it shut and fed the log into the wood chipper. Billy returned, though, to find a different soul in each tree, but never his wife. So he practiced, lips parting each time and secrets spilling out. When he finds her, she will be perfect. But so far, he has nothing but a pile of woodchips.

'Please don't,' the mouth says. 'I'll do anything.'

'Be quiet and let me work.'

Over the following days, the man hacks away at the log,

carving it up, sharpening the edges. Billy shapes her slender limbs, the slight torso. Every inch worked smooth with a file and sandpaper.

He hangs up the last tool and takes a sip from his mug. The eyes closed, lids twitching as he places a hand on the pointed shoulder. A finger moves and a knee lifts.

'Are you done?' the mouth says, turning the head.

'See for yourself.'

It sits up on the bench and looks down at the golden whirls on its body.

'This is so wrong. I'm a man. A thin man with a potbelly and knobbly knees.'

Seeing its reflection in a mirror, it swings its legs towards the floorboards of the cabin.

'You're my best effort yet,' Billy says. 'Beautiful.'

It lunges at Billy, but he is ready, and he fires a nail gun through its foot, pinning it to the floor.

'I'm sorry. Please, I'll do anything.'

'Don't worry,' Billy says, holding a rag to its mouth. 'I just need one thing from you.'

The eyes open to sunlight, taking a moment, before finding Billy sat on a stump, nail gun in hand. Her body laid out in the middle of the circle.

'This is where I found her,' Billy says, waving the gun across the clearing. 'I never had a chance to…'

He drops the nail gun to the floor and steps over to her body.

'Just let me say goodbye…'

The head nods and he kneels down beside her.

'I'm so sorry Hazel,' he says, slipping an arm around her neck. 'I couldn't let you go.'

Her hand lifts to squeeze his arm.

Billy leans down to kiss her on the lips, a soft touch, before going in again. The other arm swings out and knocks him to the ground.

He wakes to the smell of gasoline, tied to one of the stumps as Hazel stands before him, a lit match in hand.

'Wherever she is,' the mouth says. 'She deserves better than this.'

#

James has been writing for about twenty years, uncovering the absurd in the everyday. His stories have previously been published by *Silk + Smoke*, *FlashFlood Journal* and *Ellipsis*, amongst others. James also posts occasionally at @jturner27 and bloodbonesbricks.wordpress.com.

Morkus

By Justin Eells

One morning, Nick woke up and it was there beside him in bed: a bowling ball-sized clump of gray, vein-riddled meat. Although he lived alone, Nick had long suspected another presence in his house, and now it was showing itself. Nick smiled and poked the little thing, and a mousy squeak came out of it, followed by a slurp, which made Nick laugh. It smelled of vinegar and bowling shoe.

Nick didn't know what to feed the thing, so he made eggs and toast for two. The thing fidgeted and stretched toward the plate, stood erect like a bowling pin, then shrunk back down to the shape of sourdough loaf.

"Can I make you something else?" Nick said.

The thing spread across its chair like spilled soda and slithered down to the floor where it slid over to a small brown puddle at the foot of the fridge and turned itself over and over in the slurry.

"Morkus, don't!" Nick yelled. He didn't know why he said that—"Morkus"—but the name came out of him, so Morkus the thing was.

At first, Morkus was content to stay in the house. There were enough puddles and growths to sustain him, and Nick could go to work and Thursday-night bowling and no one had any reason to believe his situation was anything but normal. Sometimes Morkus would recline all day on the ottoman like a bunch of dusty grapes, emitting occasional slurps; sometimes he'd slink out from under the sink in the shape of a floor sock, and Nick wouldn't know if Morkus had shrunk or his mind was playing tricks. The slurping was constant, as Morkus absorbed whatever nutrients he found in the nooks and crevices, but it was tolerable.

Then one morning, a few months after Morkus first appeared in Nick's bed, Nick put on his coat and Morkus wrapped himself around his calf and squeezed, not in a painful way, but an insistent way, as if to say he would not be letting go.

At first, Morkus drew some stares at work, and people occasionally poked their heads around the cubicle walls when the slurping was especially loud, but no one said anything, and Nick was still welcome at happy hour and Thursday-night bowling.

Still, it wasn't always easy. Occasionally, Morkus would get up on the breakroom table and people would shrink back. And sometimes he got in the way of Nick's bowling game. One night, during an especially bad game, Nick's ball seemed perennially destined for the gutter and he could almost smell his teammates' tepid ire as they stared at the squishy monster affixed to his leg. Peeling Morkus off didn't seem like an option. By the end of that night, Morkus's slurping was loud enough to hear over the crashing pins and hair metal blasting from the bowling alley's speakers, so Nick opted out of the usual postgame sandwich and went home. When he turned on the TV and Morkus settled in next to him on the couch, Nick looked over and realized Morkus was now so big he took up an entire cushion, and an oozy string of him dribbled down the front of the couch like snot.

The days got shorter, the air colder, and Nick stopped attending happy hour and dropped out of the bowling league. Morkus's slurps grew louder and more frequent, and Nick noticed pieces of hair and smears of dirt sticking to his nubs of flesh. Then his parents said they were coming for Christmas.

Nick made Morkus wait in a sealable plastic container while he vacuumed the floors and scrubbed the sinks and toilet. When he opened the container to let him out, Morkus gave a high-pitched, spittly whine, and Nick promised never to leave him in there again.

When they arrived, his parents were taken aback by this ball of gray flesh that smelled like a spent scouring pad and made little slurpy sounds. His mother did not approve of Morkus: "There are ways to handle such things. You don't have to live like this."

His father was more pliant: "It's not harming anything. And it doesn't require food or a litter box, so..."

"Don't tell him that! This isn't normal. This is no way for a young man to live. When did you last have a date, Nick?

Nick looked at Morkus, the size of a small refrigerator, sitting on the floor beside the recliner, and he looked at his diminished parents sitting on the couch and felt a dull pain in his gut. That night, he took Morkus in two hands and stuffed him back into the plastic bin and slid the bin under the bed.

Christmas was pleasant enough as Nick and his parents pretended life was normal and that Morkus didn't exist. After they left, Nick pulled the container out, but when he took the lid off, there was nothing inside but a moldy smell. He looked around the house, in all the closets, the basement, and under the bed. He couldn't find the little monster anywhere. He remembered his promise never to put Morkus in the container again, and how quickly he had reneged. Nick had treated Morkus unfairly, but, as he got in the shower and let the warm water wash over his body, he felt revitalized, as if this were the start of a new life.

In bed, sleep pulled on him as it hadn't in a long time, and as he sank into its velvet embrace, he heard a quiet slurping from somewhere in the pipes or the walls, or maybe from the dream world that was drawing him in. It was perfectly normal, he decided; nothing but a sound.

#

Justin Eells lives in Minneapolis and is working on a novel about a bird cult. He tweets @OneSilent_E.

The Scaredy Men

By S.E. Casey

It looks rather dull from the road. However, Maddie cries out for the lure, starved for stimulation having spent all morning in the car.

I pull over to the shoulder, tires crunching over the crispy chaff as if it were bones of small birds. The hot and arid weather clings stubbornly into the fall.

My wife sighs. However, she opens the door and the three of us exit into the dusty midday heat. Maddie runs to the entrance of the cornfield maze. It is unmanned, no one to stop her, unless one counts the scarecrow slumping on an old picnic table.

I read the sign slung over its crooked neck, a shaky scrawl in black marker.

One dollar. Children are FREE.

I fish out two bucks and stick them under the scarecrow's floppy palm hat.

Danielle rolls her eyes. We are saving for Maddie's ballet lessons and I'm the impulse spender.

"Hey, it's only fair," I shrug.

Noticing a ceramic bowl filled with matchbooks, I grab one and read its cover.

The Scaredy Man.

I flip it over.

Who am I?

Pocketing it, Danielle and I enter the maze to catch up with our daughter.

*

The stalks loom high above our heads. The foliage is heavy, pregnant with the unharvested ears of rotting dent corn.

We hit another dead end. Danielle grumbles as we double back to the last intersection. Maddie's laughter sounds somewhere ahead of us. We will catch up with her eventually. At least I hope.

Despite its inauspicious beginnings, the road visible through the gaps in the water-starved stalks, the maze has thickened and become deviously complex. We are spun around. The corn is too high and lush to see any landmarks. The sun conspires against us too. It blazes directly above making it useless as a guide.

I wipe my forehead. However, it is dry, my rough skin fraying to the touch.

*

Deeper and deeper we go.

Several times we had tried doubling back. However, the turns negotiated only moments before seem different as if the maze changes behind us. No matter the strategy, we spiral further in.

Maddie is gone, her giggles and hoots lost to the field. She deserves her freedom, not to have her fun curbed by us. Danielle is sullen. However, she seems to have accepted it, at least no longer calling her name.

There is nothing we can do. We had been warned.

One dollar. Children are FREE.

Children are FREE.

I look up at the taunting moon, full and lonely in the vacant sky. But much like the sun, it offers no solace.

Listening for sounds of the road prove fruitless as well. Even if there were a honk or a crash of an accident, the steady beating of the drums drowns it out. Deep and persistent, they thrum like a heartbeat.

I tap my finger on the cover of the matchbook, mouthing its words to the rhythm.

The Scaredy Man.

"We should split up." Danielle's voice is raspy and tired.

I nod. So insufferably dry here, my mouth is too parched to speak.

*

The ground crunches beneath my feet, the discarded husks shed from the stalks having ossified in the heat. Loose kernels calcified into little sharp teeth bite into the soles of my shoes.

The walls of vegetation tighten around me. Although robust, pushing me back whenever I brush them, they are dehydrated and brittle. I had hoped the night would produce a quenching dew, but it seems hotter than the day.

The moon blinks behind the black burlap canvases waving in the gales. But it isn't burlap, rather the scratchy night sky pulled down and sliced into ribbons.

There are no forks in the path, no choices to be made. Points that should have been intersections are cut off as if giant hay bales had been rolled into place. The closing window above and the rippling bands of night allow so little light it makes it impossible to tell.

Who am I?

I clutch the matchbook tightly, grateful for its wisdom.

The drums thunder, vibrations shaking the chalky pollen from the stalks. My throat and nose close up. I want to sneeze but can't, as if the oppressive aridity has dried out my sinuses.

I stumble forward on shaky legs until I can't go further, a solid wall in front of me. The tattered sky is gone, the canopy closed overhead. Drenched in a dry, starchy darkness, the parched vegetation presses around me like I am a baby in a straw cocoon.

I tear a stick from the matchbook. Without any humidity in the air, it lights on the first strike. In the phosphorus flash, button eyes leer at me, mouths slashed into frozen screams thirstily gape.

The match falls from my paralyzed hand. I watch it bounce on the withered pillow of shells at my feet several times before slipping between the gaps in the loose chaff.

Darkness engulfs me again. But it is short-lived, a dull orange glow blooming around me. In the swelling light, the menacing faces return. Eyes burn like coals and mouths smolder. The incendiary drums beat faster, climaxing into a violent crescendo.

Caught up in the searing updrafts, the wispy figures around me begin to rise. Propelled upwards, they silently scream, escaping the blaze. And I rise with them. Hoisted into the night, my burlap and straw self ascends over the field.

It is a beautiful sight. Embers pop and dance like drunk fireflies as a ring of fire races outward, consuming the field. The puzzle is solved, the flames reducing the maze to ash. Like a phoenix, it will grow again, another tangled configuration to be born.

And we, the solvers of the maze, will be there to defend it.

We, the transcendent gods of the field.

The scared, the scarred, and the sacred.

The Scaredy Men.

#

S.E Casey lives on the coast of Massachusetts near a lighthouse. His weird fiction has appeared in *Weirdbook, Hinnom Magazine, Vastarien,* and most recently the puppet-themed anthology, *Mannequin.* He also has an interest in reading and writing flash fiction. His flash stories have appeared in many online publications, a listing which can be found at www.secaseyauthor.wordpress.com.

PHANTOMS

"It is far harder to murder a phantom
than a reality."
– Virginia Woolf

Angels of Purgatory

by Chris Panatier

The doctor says it's something called *retinitis pigmentosa* and there's nothing he can do, nothing anyone can do. He's yammering about how gene therapy is still years off, says the bright side is that other senses may sharpen. Through the window, I can see my car in the parking lot, though it's no more than a blurry teal jellybean. I know I'll have to quit driving soon.

Back home, I cry over a photograph of Samantha like always. She was seven, just starting to make the world feel her. Now she's fuzzy around the edges. The day's coming that I'll go to look and not recognize. At some point after that, I won't see anything. If I can't see her, will I forget?

I'm cramming to learn braille before the lights go out, trying to find a voice recognition software that knows legalese so I can keep my job. Honestly, though, I don't care. Sometimes, I wish I were my eyesight's companion, fading then gone. Blip.

Time passes more slowly when you dread. I see blobs. Light and dark. I stopped going to the office last week. Groceries are delivered now. I filled a glass with vinegar when I thought I was pouring juice and now everything has its place. I hold Samantha but can no longer see her.

Inevitably, one morning, the sun fails to rise. I sit on my couch like a statue, the lone occupant in a world of darkness. My fingers clutch a picture frame, but I can't be sure if it's her. I rage at my idiocy for not placing it away from the other photographs in anticipation of my blindness. It matters that I hold the right picture.

It matters.

I exist in a world between. A haunt in my old life, an alien in the new, fully in neither. Senses do sparkle some. With repetition, my fingers map and remember. Scents become rich and complex—loaded with information that I can't decode. I am surprised by my ears' burgeoning sensitivity. They tell me distance, mass, even material—how sound bounces from a painted wall as opposed to the wooden floor. A cluster of leaves drops into the grass to tell me that autumn has come.

October ends with children at my door. I offer the bowl forward. They dig for what they want with tiny hands that are not hers.

I wake one night to a roar and spring from my bed, rushing to the window as if I can still see through it. The sound is deafening, like a dump truck emptying gravel. I ask my digital assistant if there is a storm. There isn't. I pace my room hoping it will pass. It doesn't. I brave the front door, the porch. I enter the sound and experience what I imagine it's like at the mouth of a cave with bats streaking by.

I hear the friction of one thing giving way to another, the violence of molecules buffeted. And I realize what I am hearing. It is the leaves themselves, their edges cutting the air. I hear them together at first, swarming like starlings, but with some concentration I can discern the individuals spinning to the ground. At this, the roar subsides. I push my senses outward. I hear the gentle unclasping of their stems from the limb and the thunder of their collisions with the earth. From where they come, to the place they rest, they paint a picture.

In the coming days, I learn the sounds of blood pushing through veins, spiders spinning out silk, blooms on the knockout roses closing. Rays of sunlight warming the carpet.

I hear it all.

And amid the noise, there are contours of another place—a landscape somewhere just out of reach—emerging. There are voices, muffled and whispering, puckish. They gallop, hand-in-hand, little herds.

I cry out—ask who they are, where they are, where they are going. Is Samantha with them? Some slow at my voice, stop and gaze about, but continue on. I listen, mapping the place where they run.

Early in the morning, I wake and roll upright on the couch. When I project into the other place, there are no more whispers, no more galloping herds. Across what sounds like a sun-drenched meadow, there is a small group gathered and waiting. I reach for them. Walk in their direction. They shuffle to one side. I alter my course in turn.

In the living room, my body bumps the shelf, and I hear the clap of a picture frame fallen forward. I snatch it up.

The group disperses. Tiny heads bounce into the setting sun as they make for the meadow's edge. The landscape in dusk recedes beyond the reach of my hearing.

One after another, each ear adjusts—the faint pop that comes with a change in pressure. Sounds no longer pierce and boom. Sitting with Samantha, the world is quiet again.

#

Chris Panatier lives in Dallas, Texas, with his wife, daughter, and a fluctuating herd of animals resembling dogs (one is almost certainly a goat). He writes, "plays" the drums, and draws album covers for metal bands. As a lawyer, he goes after companies that poison people. His short fiction has appeared in or is forthcoming from *Metaphorosis, The Molotov Cocktail, Ghost Parachute, The Ginger Collect, Tales to Terrify, Trembling with Fear, Ellipsis Zine, Defenestration* and others. *The Phlebotomist,* Chris's debut novel, comes out in September 2020 via Angry Robot. Plays himself on Twitter @chrisjpanatier.

The Black Cat's Breakfast

by Chandra Steele

I awoke to find the cat motionless. I bent my head near to its mouth. There was a steady hiss and return of breath.

I'd had a restless night. I'd been reading before bed and the characters' realities mixed with my own through the shallow waves of my waking and dreaming. I shook them out of my ears and eyes. That Murakami can really mess with your head.

I shuffled down the hall to the bathroom. I checked my reflection and ran my hand down my face for a second opinion. Same old Genichi Sawamura. Not everything was the same though. I didn't detect the smell of coffee that had unfailingly accompanied my waking for the three years I'd been married to Keiko.

I put on jeans and a T-shirt and went downstairs. A note was in the spot where breakfast usually was.

Had to leave extra early.
Fend for yourself today!
XOXO,
Keiko

There was a café near the train station that I'd been meaning to try. Today was destined to be the day. I tugged on a sweater and went out into the bright autumn light.

Barely anyone was on the street since it was past the morning commute. But as a writer, I'm accustomed to a different schedule.

The café was between a newsagent and a florist. I opened the door to a light jingle from a small string of temple bells. The shop was bright and airy. Not spacious, but the matching blond wood of the vertically laid floor, the low counter, and the few tables and chairs gave that appearance.

"Welcome," the elderly proprietor said.

"Good morning," I said as I suddenly regretted not ducking into the newsagent's first for a paper. At home, I slowly turn over the pages rather than listening to the sound of my own chewing.

"Can I take a table, please, even though it's just me?" With no other customers, I was pretty sure it wasn't going to be a problem.

"Of course," the shopkeeper said.

"I just made some rice porridge. It's my specialty," he said as I sat down. While it did imbue the shop with a homey smell, it wasn't what was on my mind.

"I'll actually have toast and eggs and coffee," I said. I realized it was what the characters in the book I was reading were eating before I lost them to sleep.

"Easy enough. Scrambled? Omelet-style?"

"Let's go with omelet-style."

He went behind the counter and soon there was the hiss of the percolator and the sound of eggs in a hot skillet. The plate and a large mug of coffee, both steaming, were soon before me. I dove in.

"It's a nice day," the shopkeeper said. "Perfect autumn weather."

Ah, the chatty type. Not really my specialty since I spend most of my day holed up by choice. Even when Keiko comes home, I'm more in the listener role in our conversations.

I could feel him waiting for a response.

"My wife left me without breakfast today."

"Ha," the old man chuckled. "Since I've opened this shop, my wife never makes me breakfast."

"How long have you been open?" I didn't want to get into talk of marital discord, however minor. It's part of what I like about Keiko. Even if we've been arguing, nothing affects the flow of daily living. Breakfast gets made, groceries get bought, garbage gets taken out, the cat gets fed.

The cat. I'd forgotten about him in favor of my own stomach. Suddenly I couldn't take another bite. Tiredness swept my entire being like I was slowly being dragged out to sea.

"I don't know what's come over me. I must lie down for a moment."

"I keep a cot in the back for that very reason," the shopkeeper said. "When you get to be my age, these moments happen more and more."

He walked me to a corner in the back. As soon as I hit the sling of fabric, I was in a kitchen that was mine but not, the way it is in dreams. A man had his back to me. He was spooning up bits of hard-boiled egg, a few melon pieces at the edge of his plate. Something about him was familiar. He had a stocky build, thick white-flecked black hair. I walked around to see him from the front. Haruki Murakami.

"This is very strange, you being in my kitchen. Well, sort of my kitchen," I said to him.

He continued chewing. "I can't be in sort of your kitchen," he said very matter-of-factly when he was finished.

"I find it odd for you of all people to say that. People are sort of everything in your books."

"But not in real life," he said.

"This is a dream," I said.

"This is real life," he said. "I am eating breakfast."

"I had toast and eggs and coffee," I said. I don't know why. Maybe I thought he'd recognize this signpost from his own work.

"Scrambled or omelet-style?" he asked.

"Omelet-style."

He nodded.

Finally I said: "Have you seen a cat around?"

He looked me directly in the eye, which I realized he hadn't been doing for our entire conversation. My eyelids opened.

The shopkeeper was washing pots. I sat up and began to apologize.

"No need, no need," he said. He'd been really understanding of the whole strange episode. He patted me on the back and I took some bills out of my wallet and bid him goodbye.

When I got home in the kitchen there was a plate of half-eaten breakfast that had the exact amount and placement of food as Murakami's. The cat was sitting on the stool, as sleek and black and alive as ever, licking bits of egg from its whiskers and staring me straight in the eye.

\#

Chandra Steele's work can be found in *Paper Darts, Vol. 1 Brooklyn, McSweeney's Internet Tendency, The Scofield, Litro Magazine, Newtown Literary, Meat for Tea: The Valley Review,* and *The Molotov Cocktail*. Rick Moody once said she wrote the best description of a racetrack he has ever read. She has never been to a racetrack. More of her writing can be found at chandrasteele.com.

Mandible

by Phillip E. Dixon

I found the jaw beneath a corner table in the café. The pewter glint of a dental filling caught my eye while I swept. I picked him up and ran my finger lightly across his worn molars, tickling him by accident—he writhed happily at my touch. I should have put him in the bin of forgotten things, but the jaw was lonely and I found myself sliding him into my purse instead.

Our courtship was a ginger affair. I wore him delicately around my collar like a necklace to keep him close, which he enjoyed. His masseter muscles gripped my throat tenderly, keeping him in place as I went about my routines. I laid him on my pillow at night and he nuzzled my hair while I slept. Stubble grew, so I shaved him, but it was different from shaving my legs. The angles were peculiar and I navigated the cleft of his chin poorly, cutting him. Blood welled and he drooled with pain. I wept, horrified at what I'd done. I wiped the saliva from his bottom lip and offered my cheek to his incisors, but he didn't resent me.

In time, I found myself wanting more. So, I slipped out of my lower jaw and picked him up. We both trembled as he settled into place, his medial softly meeting my lateral. My tongue ran over his bottom lip, thrilling me with its fullness.

Finally, we masticated.

We chewed and gnawed, slurping with grace, crafting bolus after bolus in rhythm together. We ate the hottest curries and swallowed the darkest chocolates. Ice cubes melted slowly, trapped inside our gleefully numbed mouth. We crunched pistachios and suckled green tea bags. We gargled and we spit, and every sensation was fresh again.

We spoke new words together, our different lips meeting in unfamiliar parings, stumbling on our first syllables until plosive firecrackers and sibilant cascades shook our quivering face. We cried out and sang, sending spittle waves through the air. We laughed, our mouth a hinge of joy.

Sometimes we clenched, yes, but I always wore him proudly.

Sometimes our teeth ground, but he always jutted his scarred chin with devotion.

I learned to shave him properly, faithfully, so I never noticed the grey in his beard. He was much older than me. While my canines remained sharp, his shattered. Where my bite was deep, his turned shallow. My lips stayed tender and ripe, while his became cankerous and pale.

Eventually, he asked me to unlock him, to free myself, but I refused. I'd never loved him more. We sat in the bedroom together until he fell slack and loose, dangling death from my face.

Yet I am still with him, and he with me.

The stubble is gone now, and his skin has sloughed away. I carved a nick in his barren chin so I won't forget where his scar used to be. My tongue probes his solitary teeth and the hollow sockets in between. I taste for memories. I try to make what words I can—to tell him that I still love him—but my tongue falls through the bottom of our mouth, dangling listlessly below the cold, naked bone.

#

Phillip E. Dixon is a writer, musician, and college English instructor living in Las Vegas. He holds an MFA in Writing from Lindenwood University, and a BA in English Literature from Pacific Lutheran University. He plays guitar and mandolin, speaks poor German, and is definitely stuck in traffic right now.

Day Ninety-One

by Jo Withers

When the food ran out, the government started putting supplements in the water.

We were never hungry again. The water incorporated a perfect balance of vitamins and nutrients for energy and growth. It was the colour and consistency of the stuff that pours from a tuna can when it drains, faintly metallic in odour with an oily sheen, but we got used to it and it was satisfying. After a while, people forgot that they'd ever had to eat. The water gave us everything we needed.

Five years later, the problems started. At first, the government refused to accept they'd caused the deformities. They blamed the lower classes, said it was drug abuse or genetic abnormalities, anything except the water. But over time, the incidents increased until one in every hundred kids was born that way.

When they first emerged, they didn't look much different. But they grew like crazy. They had a full set of teeth by day ten and by day fifteen they were walking, although not like any kid you'd seen before. With hands and feet on the floor, they scuttled and pulled themselves along like a half-squashed beetle, joints clicking and creaking as they progressed.

By day forty, they were going through their teenage phase and there was no reasoning with them. Most families found it easiest to lock them away, releasing them again on day forty-five when the perplexities of puberty had waned.

Of course, everyone worried where this rapid growth would lead. It didn't take long before the parents' worst fears were realised, and their children began to die. It was a sickening death too. Most of them would begin to stiffen around day eighty. From then, rigor mortis would gradually possess their still-breathing bodies until finally, on day ninety, only their eyeballs could move in tiny flickering circles inside their petrified frames.

The parents were distraught, but the government found the situation convenient. The children were born, lived a short life and died. Their life-cycles played out within people's homes without encroaching on the overloaded health care system and there was no need for research into such a short-lived problem. In a gesture of goodwill, they extended maternity and paternity pay to parents of those affected so that they could spend the entire three months of their offspring's life at home. Everything was reasonable and contained and the government saw no reason to intervene.

Then, suddenly, they began to evolve. Some of them didn't stiffen at eighty days old, some of them started to survive. But there was a catch. If they made it to ninety days, they needed to feed, no, to feast. That's when the killings started—dogs, cows, sheep, people. All found in the same way, with the same horrific scars on their lower backs where their marrow had been extracted.

The government acted immediately, started monitoring the babies born in hospitals and taking the ones away that showed abnormal growth in the first twenty-four hours. No one knew what happened to them, but they never returned.

A nasty period of mass hysteria followed where people tried to beat the system and risked delivering their babies at home rather than having them taken away. Women stopped going for prenatal scans and tried to disguise their pregnancies. Childbirth had gone underground.

After she was born, we were both in denial for the first few hours. Hidden away in our family's cabin, it was a mercifully easy birth, but nothing was simple after. Laura tried so hard to feed her on the first day, but she had no interest in her mother's milk; all she wanted was the water. By the next day, it was obvious she was one of them.

That first cycle, we just made the most of every day. She couldn't talk but she'd nestle against us and we felt that most primitive bond between parent and child. As day ninety approached, we made her a bed in the woodshed, tied a sheep inside and left her there. On day ninety-one, I held Laura in the cabin whilst horrendous preternatural screeching sounded from the woodshed.

Later, when we opened the door, we thought she was dead. The adult daughter we had left there that morning lay on the floor, ribs split down the middle like some interrupted autopsy. Laura was crying and screaming for our dead daughter and everything felt hopeless, when suddenly, I saw a small hand move inside the ribcage. As I looked inside, I saw our daughter, newborn again, nestled inside her old self—a new baby in a basket of her old bones. I tried not to look at the shrunken sheep skin in the corner as Laura tenderly lifted our baby daughter into her arms again, kissed her head and called her 'Miracle' as she had the first time she was born.

Over the years, we've learnt what works, how many rabbits or squirrels I need to catch and keep for her on day ninety-one. It's wonderful afterwards, we take it in turns to hold her for the first time again.

They track us down every so often. They sent out a health visitor first. When she didn't come back, they sent a government official. People can keep her sustained the longest, if she doesn't drain them fully the first time we can keep them alive to last another cycle. I suppose they'll send the police next. When she's finished with them, it will be time to move on.

We're on day twelve again, now. In a few days she'll be walking. Today, she reached up and pulled herself onto my lap for the first time this cycle. I took a photograph and stuck it in her baby book, all dimples and blonde curls. Through all her cycles, we'll build memories just like any other childhood, and like all parents, we'll love her unconditionally.

#

Jo Withers writes short fiction for children and adults. Her work has featured in *The Caterpillar, Milk Candy Review, Bath Flash Fiction* and *Reflex Fiction* amongst other places. One of her pieces has also been selected for *Best Microfiction 2020*.

The Places We Go Where Others May Not Follow

by Liz Schriftsteller

I'm not allowed in the room at the top of the stairs.

My mother has the only key, and when she goes inside, she goes alone. "What do you keep in there?" I'd ask, but the answer was never the same.

"Books," she said, "A whole library full of them, with a wingback chair for reading." Or, "Wine," when I asked again, "Full of exotic vintages and dust covered bottles dating back to the 1900s."

Each story only piqued my curiosity.

I'd try to steal a glimpse inside, but she slipped through the door too quickly for my eyes. One day I caught a whiff of salt-sea air and the call of a gull before she pulled the door shut. When she came out again a few hours later, her skin was burnt, her kiss salty-sour from limes and tequila. She giggled and sang and let me have ice cream for dinner.

My father was not amused.

He argued with her in hushed tones after he put me to bed.

Angry whispers crept down the hall, farther than he intended.

"You can't keep doing this, Sharon." He hissed her name, like a tea kettle about to burst. I listened at the door, waiting for her answer.

"Don't be so dramatic. She barely even notices."

"*I* notice. You're up there every day, and for longer each time."

"You're one to talk." Her voice hitched, from a hiccup or sob, I couldn't tell which. "When was the last time you spent an evening home with your family? *I'll be home late, Shar. Gonna stop off with the guys, Shar.* You're not the only one who needs their alone time."

There was silence, and then a murmuring I could not decipher.

"I'll stop," she said.

But she didn't.

At first, she was gone only a few minutes, popping in and out when she thought she wouldn't be caught. Minutes stretched into hours. Then one day, she went in after breakfast and didn't come out until dark.

Calling for her proved fruitless. I screamed until my voice was hoarse but she either couldn't hear me or didn't care. In any case, she never came.

I was reading at the foot of the staircase when at last the door burst open. She vaulted down the stairs and scooped me up her arms in a tight embrace. I squirmed against her wet cheeks, protesting. When she finally let me go, I could see her hair held flecks of grey. On her face: a scar I'd never seen before, cut deep into her chin, already white with age.

The door to the room hung open, its gaping maw bearing down on me from the top of the upper landing. I couldn't see much beyond the door, except for a lone cardinal that darted across a clear blue sky.

The question of what lay behind the door consumed me.

Every day I interrogated my mother regarding its contents. Her lies grew more outlandish until at last her patience wore thin.

"Inside is a house just like this one, except backwards, like a mirror. I have a daughter there, who's just like you, but better, because she never asks me questions and always does as she's told."

I grimaced. "Well, why don't you stay there forever then, if she's so much better."

"I have," she said, her eyes wide. "In fact, I'm not even me, I'm the mother from the other side, trying desperately to get back to my loving family, and away from you." She snapped closed the book she was reading and stuck it under her arm, heading for the top of the stairs.

My father and I watched her go. "She doesn't really have another family in there, does she?" I asked, once the door was shut behind her.

He took a sip of whisky, swirling the ice in his glass in lieu of comment.

"I mean, she clearly doesn't want one family. I can't imagine she'd have another."

His lips curled into a smile in spite of himself.

"What do you think is in there?"

"Dreams," he said, after another long pull from his glass. "That's where she keeps her dreams."

I stared at him, not knowing where to begin. I'd always assumed the room was hers and hers alone, but another thought emerged, a question I had never asked.

"Have you ever been inside?"

He smiled. "I'm one of the few things she ever let out."

We sat in silence for a long time after that, more questions than answers swirling through my head. I begged my father to let me stay up until she came out again, but he tucked me into bed against my yawning protests.

That was the last time I saw her.

"We should go after her," I told my father. "You saw her scar. It's dangerous, we need to bring her back."

He shook his head. "It doesn't work like that. Even if you could get the door open, there's no telling where it would lead; it takes you where you want to go, not where others have gone."

"She'll be there," I insisted, "Because I want to go where I can find her."

"Not if she doesn't want to be found."

I glared at him.

"Trust me," he said, "I've tried. There are places we go where others may not follow. She'll come back when she's good and ready."

I've been good and ready these last three years, but the door has stayed shut.

Tonight, there is a new door at the end of the hall. I don't remember seeing it before, but unlike my mother's room, this door is unlocked. I hold the knob and look over at my father's crumpled frame, asleep in front of the TV and clutching his empty whisky glass.

We all retreat in our own ways, and I am no exception.

#

Liz Schriftsteller hails from North Carolina but these days 'home' is anywhere the Wi-Fi automatically connects. Her published fiction includes works found in *Daily Science Fiction*, *Phobos* magazine, and *The Arcanist*. Follow her at www.lizschriftsteller.wordpress.com or on Twitter @LizSchriftstell.

Crop Circles

by Christina Dalcher

The stealing happened even before, back when celluloid was king and you could buy a 36-shot roll of Kodak color film for a few bucks. That was a small-scale problem; people spent their shots with care on family portraits, newborns in cradles, birthday boys and girls. Occasionally, a tourist in Paris might snap a picture of the shitty Pompidou Center and manage to catch a stranger in the lens, and that stranger would look as though he suffered an inexplicable accident. But that was before and this is now. There are so many more pictures. Selfies, panoramas, videos, accidental bursts of a hundred from the pressure of a lingering thumb.

And so many croppings.

Jamie is one of the first (but there will be millions more), and he starts feeling it on Monday morning. He doesn't actually feel it; he sees and hears it when his right hand detaches itself from his wrist and falls to the pavement with a dead thump, still holding on to the leather portfolio he's hauling to his next appointment. His wrist twitched a moment ago, something to do with tendons or overuse or that damned carpal tunnel syndrome, but this isn't twitching. This is a hand lying on the sidewalk. This is a piece of him, cut off from the rest and lost.

He watches the hand dissolve, first opaque, then transparent, then spread into particles fine as dust motes, leaving only the sweat-stained handle of his portfolio.

While Jamie walks to work (or was walking—now Jamie is howling on the pavement, groping at the spot where his severed hand used to be), Marybeth pinches and swipes the surface of her tablet, on which glows a near-perfect night shot of St. Mark's—near perfect because some bothersome passerby with a portfolio case the size of Montana stepped into the frame in the millisecond before she tapped, and now she has a killer shot of the cathedral with a fucking hand at the right edge, holding onto a portfolio that ruined the lines of the thing. She could retake the shot, but not with a hard deadline of noon. So Marybeth pinches the cropping rectangle in with her stylus, and somewhere five blocks north, Jamie's hand falls to the ground and dissolves, and that's that.

Marybeth, meanwhile, has just enough time left to see her edited masterpiece before Mike McAdams puts the finishing touches on his Great Wall of China album, pulling the rectangular crop lines inward so as to get rid of the annoying half-head of a woman at the bottom of the frame, leaving only his smiling wife and son and miles of stone. Marybeth sniffs once, and her brain registers the fact that it's no longer attached to the part of her doing the sniffing. Then it doesn't register anything else.

Wendy McAdams comes into her husband's home office with a tray of chocolate biscuits and tea, all of which end up on the floor when she notices her husband doesn't exist from the waist down. She was working on her own tweaks in the kitchen, putting the finishing touches on the family's annual Christmas photo. They'd taken the kids up to Crystal Lake and posed on a flat rock above the water, but goddammit if Mike's legs didn't seem to go on forever, taking up half the frame. "Easy peasy," she said, and brought the cropping frame in tighter. And a little tighter after that, just for balance. Now Mike's lower half, splattered with tea and bits of chocolate biscuit, consists of two deflated khaki pant legs, size 36 long.

Wendy will wake up one morning with much shorter hair on one side because of last Tuesday's gallery opening when Jamie had to ask her three times to move aside so he could get the artist—and only the artist—in the publicity shot. Wendy McAdams is a habitual photo-bomber, and so she will lose first her right ear, then her left, and various other parts over the coming months. Jamie will work expensive editing software with his nondominant hand until he has to relearn the process using his feet. And Marybeth won't be doing much of anything because there's rather little you can do without a head, even if you are Architectural Digest's number-one stringer on the East Coast.

Some rumors will spread, stories of island tribes and desert nomads who still possess ten fingers and ten toes. They're just rumors, unproven and undocumented because these remaining intact people have never allowed themselves to be photographed. A silly way of thinking, really, as if the click of a camera lens could steal some part of a person's soul.

#

Christina Dalcher wrote some flash for *The Molotov Cocktail* and turned it into a novel called *VOX*. Find her in all the usual hiding places @CVDalcher. Or under a bed. Or in a dark closet re-reading a tattered copy of *The Shining*.

What the Crows Said

by Erin Fingerhut

I started feeding the crows when I was nine. I loved the way they looked at me like they were thinking things through. Weighing my heart, or my soul. I hoped they wouldn't find me wanting.

Corvids. Big, black, glossy. Bossy. Smartest birds in the world. By the time I was eleven, they would bring me gifts in return. Pebbles. Buttons. Nuts and screws. Shiny bits of broken glass. Things I was sure people lost, like a tiny little silver ring, one time, and a rusty old set of keys.

Last fall, at twelve, I had to leave school on account of the seizures. I don't remember the first one. I was in the yard, spreading sunflower seeds for the crows. They were heavy in the trees, watching, weirdly quiet. In a flurry of black feathers they flew from their branches, screaming, and circled my head. I only had a second to be scared, and then I was waking up in the hospital. Mama was at work and our neighbor, Joe, says it's a lucky thing he heard those crows because who knew how long I would have been lying out there, seizing. I could have died. Everybody said so.

After the diagnosis, I couldn't go to school anymore. I can't say I missed it. It was kinda my fault, how mean the other kids were, calling me 'freak' all the way back to kindergarten. It took too long to realize not everyone saw the colors I did. How everything pulsed with its own light. I didn't know not to talk about it. After the seizures, Mama was almost relieved, sure all my talk of colors and lights was the epilepsy peeking its gnarly head out before making its big move.

Mama had to take another job to pay for my medication. Sarah, the home nurse sent to watch over me, was nice enough, but she'd be more apt to tell you who was who on the TV than what I was doing out in the yard all day.

This spring, the crows started bringing me different kinds of treasures. Scraps of newspaper. Old coffee cups with logos and company names all over them. Once, two big, mean-looking birds, black and shiny like rainbows in oil, dropped an old rusted license plate practically on my head. It made such a clatter on the metal patio table Sarah actually came running. I kind of missed the shiny pretty things, but collected the papers like I did everything else.

When the first sinkhole appeared at the edge of town, I realized the crows were trying to talk to me. From what the news said, a whole trailer park was swallowed up inside. Without a trace. I made Sarah take me. She wouldn't admit it, but she was as curious as me. Scared too, maybe. I know I was.

I got close enough to see the giant hole, big as a football field, rimmed in a pulsing red like the stove burner turned up high. Pulsing with an anger I could feel.

After, the crows brought more paper. Discarded shopping lists. Parking tickets. I took to smoothing them out on the patio table, corners held down with pebbles and other crow treasures. The birds were insistent. They'd land by my hand, peck at the paper. Swivel their heads, wait for me to understand.

I had another seizure. Sarah came out when she heard the crows. They were pecking at my hands, my arms and legs. She thought they were trying to kill me.

When it was over, I saw the crow papers in a new light. Letters would stand out with their own ominous glow. I'd write them down in neat rows, like a word jumble. I tried to get Mama's help. She just smiled with tired, sad eyes and quietly closed her bedroom door. She was so sure the epilepsy scrambled my brains she couldn't believe anything I wanted to tell her about crows and secret messages.

It was Sarah that figured it out. She was checking on me as I sat dejected out in the yard, staring at my page of letters. "West," she said all matter of fact as she walked by. I about fell over. Once I saw that, I could pick out others. "Fly." "Wing." Later I saw, "Deep." "Branch." "Dark."

My favorite crow, a little sassy one, brought two dirty, old scrabble tiles, dropped them right in my lap. She cocked her head, looked at me with her bright, little eye. I turned the letters over in my hand.

"Go."

In the end, Mama didn't need much convincing. Cave-ins, sinkholes, tremors and quakes—there was a news story every day. A town gone. Near us, or to the East. We hadn't seen my grandparents for years, on purpose, but they were "West."

When my town went, it was the start of something new. We saw it on a live news broadcast, standing slack-jawed in a tiny Wichita living room. Something like the earth itself had come alive in a huge roiling mass. Boulder teeth and pine tree spikes, angry red molten eyes. With a mighty shrug, concrete broke apart and rolled right off. And just like that, our southern Indiana town, barely visible on a map, was gone.

It wasn't long before the crows started gathering again, out in the yard. I fed them berries and cheese, and they brought me their gifts of words. "Deep." "Dark." "West."

"Go."

My grandparents wouldn't listen, so it was just me and Mama. I didn't know where we would go. I didn't know if it would be "West" enough. All I knew was that I was going to listen to what the crows said.

#

Erin Fingerhut is a writer of sci-fi, horror, and genre-bending short stories and novellas. She moonlights in advertising, reads books, spins records and watches way too much TV.

The Unopened Bar of Chocolate

by Steve Campbell

I keep an unopened bar of chocolate under my bed. I take it out every now and again—usually after Mom's given me a telling off—and run my fingers along the wrapper, but I haven't opened it. Not yet.

I probably should explain.

There are three rules: I have to be given the item, I can't just take it. Then, I have to eat it—food and drink work best but as long as I can swallow it, I can use it. And then I have to want whatever comes next to happen.

The first time was an accident. I wanted to play football and Dad wanted me to finish my supper. He always did the cooking. I shoved the flakes of fish around my plate and grumbled under my breath. I wished he would leave me alone.

Dad didn't come home from work the next day. Mom said he was shacked up with some slag he worked with. When I realised what I'd done, I tried to put things back to how they were, but it was too late.

I was more careful after that. There were almost no more

accidents.

During science class, Mr Stanley launched a piece of chalk at me from the front of the class. "QUIET!" he spat. "You're not here to talk. You're here to listen." The chalk bounced off the side of my face and landed on the floor by my feet. The laughter in the classroom stung as much as the mark on my cheek. I slipped the chalk into my pocket when the bell rang for breaktime.

At home, I crunched the chalk with the back of a teaspoon and stirred the powder into a glass of milk.

During assembly the next morning there was one seat in the hall that didn't have a teacher in it. The headmaster kept looking over at it while we screeched our way through the hymns.

I practised on some of my classmates while Mr. Stanley was away. I got better at it. He came back to school the next term. He explained to us what asthma was, and about how his doctor had discovered an allergy to chalk. "After all these years of teaching and writing on blackboards, who'd have guessed it?" he said in a hoarse voice.

Last week, me and Mom were on holiday. Mom's new boyfriend, Ray, came with us. It was the first time we'd been back to the caravan without Dad. Mom said she wanted me to be good, that she was thinking of letting Ray move in with us. The holiday was a practice run, she said.

Ray swayed in his seat as he waved his pint glass at me. Splashes of beer landed on the table.

"Make yourself scarce, there's a good lad," Ray grunted. His tongue was like a pink slug, poking out over teeth that were the colour of piss. "Unless you wanna drink?" He cackled. The spit at the corners of his mouth stretched between his lips.

We'd come to the caravan park clubhouse every night since we'd been here. I usually had a packet of crisps and a lemonade. Mom and Ray drank beer while we listened to a man dressed as a woman sing Dolly Parton songs.

"Leave him be, Ray. He's only a boy." Mom's eyes were half-closed but she managed a smile in my direction.

"Never did me any harm." Ray snorted. "Make a man of him. Put hair on his chest." The last word came out as *chesss*.

When Ray pawed at Mom's hair and lapped at her ear, she threw her head back and squealed. I couldn't hear what Ray was muttering over the chorus from '9 to 5'.

"Go on, then." I nodded at Ray's glass. "I'll have a drink."

"Cheeky git!" He pushed his drink across the table, "Here, finish this. I ain't buying you a full one." I peered down the glass, past the rings of foam gathered around the inside, to the murky liquid in the bottom. "Now go and find something to do," he said.

Mom tutted as I got up.

Why don't you find something to do, I wanted to say. I didn't though. But I wanted to.

I took the drink back to our caravan and sat on the steps with it. The beer smelt like garden but tasted like soap. I shuddered as I gulped down the first mouthful, then I belched. The taste came back up and swirled around inside my mouth. I took another swig. And then another. When the glass was empty, I rested it against the steps and kicked my heel through it. I hid the shards in the space below the caravan, where Dad used to keep his fishing rods.

Then I went inside to wait.

I must have nodded off because it was dark when Mom woke me up. Her eyes looked sad and she had matted hair stuck to her face.

"It's Ray," she said. "There was trouble at the club. Oh, God." She started crying. There was blood on her hands and arms.

The next morning, before we left to visit Ray in hospital, Mom bought a teddy bear holding a pink heart, and a bar of chocolate from the caravan park shop. When I sat down next to Ray's bed, and saw the mass of bandages where his face used to be, I wondered how long it would be before he could eat something other than soup again. The bandages were covered in red patches where blood had leaked through. Red slug juice.

Mom looked from the bandages to the chocolate and then back to the bandages. "You have this, love," she said, handing me the chocolate.

I didn't say anything. I smiled a thank you and dropped it into my pocket. I put it under my bed when I got home.

I haven't opened the chocolate. Not yet.

#

Est. 1973, Steve Campbell is currently working on a novel. He somehow finds time to manage *Ellipsis Zine* lit magazine and mostly writes in short sentences. Steve is tall.

Threes

by Christina Dalcher

There were five of them, five bottles of beer on the fridge shelf just behind the orange juice. Five. I know, because I bought a six-pack and drank one, and I can still do math. Janie kissed me in the morning, said I tied one on and forgot.

"There were five," I said over coffee. "Five."

Little Emma, our youngest, held up a pudgy hand and spread the middle fingers to make a W. "Three!" It was her first and only word.

"That's right, honey," I said, pulling her pinky and thumb up to meet the others. "There are three now. But there were five last night."

She wrinkled her nose and put her hand down. "Three."

We all—stupidly—laughed.

*

Work was work, same old-same old, at least until Bud stormed into my office while I was shrugging on my overcoat and getting ready to leave for my five-o'clock with our top client.

"Where the hell were you, Jack?" Normally Bud was fine, good guy, easy to work for. He didn't sound good or easy right now.

I hesitated long enough to miss my beat.

"They waited a fucking hour for you. An hour, Jack. You don't answer your phone when a man calls?"

I held out my phone. "No messages, no texts."

Bud shook his head. "No job."

That was Monday, the day the beer went missing, my phone number changed to 333-3333, a client meeting got pushed up by a couple hours, and I watched my train leave from a platform I wasn't on.

It was a shit day, but I'd soon think of Monday as the best day of my week.

*

Janie sat hunched over the checkbook and her laptop when I finally made it home, eyes crossed and forehead creased. "What happened to the money, Jack?" She didn't wait for an answer. "It's gone. All of it."

I checked over her shoulder. Janie was wrong. The ten thousand we had in our account wasn't gone.

The statement showed we had three dollars left. "Three," I said.

Little Emma echoed me, her hand high in the air, her pinky and thumb held down so the middle fingers made a W. "Three!"

This time, none of us laughed.

*

A man does what he needs to do. He mans up, he pounds the pavement in the city and scours the job boards in the ether. He calls his old college mates and leaves pathetic, incoherent messages. And then, when he's pounded and scoured and begged everyone he knows, he waits.

While he's waiting, he counts.

72

Three eggs instead of the half-dozen in the fridge. Three chairs around the kitchen table. Three sets of plates and silverware in the drawer.

At dinner on Tuesday, I watched my wife and my girls. Janie stared down at her plate. Sarah and Melanie talked about boys and grades and dances, wondering how they would find money for new school clothes. Only Emma looked happy, bouncing in her booster seat, arranging pieces of food in perfect little piles: three peas, three bites of meatloaf, three carrot sticks.

"Enough," I said, and added more to her plate. I turned my back for a minute—no, a second—and when I turned again, there were three of everything.

Emma cocked her head, and I saw her eyes move from me to Janie to her sisters. Her lips moved while she counted.

*

I called in a favor and took out a loan to cover Sarah and Melanie's burials. Even then, things got fucked up. The bill came back for three caskets instead of two, and the obituary notice went out with the wrong time for the service. Emma sat between Janie and me in the front row of the empty chapel, her head resting on the swell of my wife's stomach. Three curlicues of blonde fell in fat loops over the black material, less like threes and more like sixes. When Emma laughed during the eulogies, I wanted to tug them taut, pull them out by the roots. My hand crept to the right, fingers stretched and tense, but when Emma stared up with wide eyes, I let that hand go limp.

*

On Saturday night at dinner, the three of us sat around food long grown cold. Little Emma bounced and giggled in her chair.

"Three," she whispered, looking from me to Janie to the growing bump under my wife's apron. "Three."

#

Christina Dalcher wrote some flash for *The Molotov Cocktail* and turned it into a novel called *VOX*. Find her in all the usual hiding places @CVDalcher. Or under a bed. Or in a dark closet re-reading a tattered copy of *The Shining*.

The Last Horizon

by Michael Carter

The world was not pretty anymore. But that's not why people no longer wanted to see. It was what came from the dark that made them wish for blindness.

The change started with acid rain, followed by blue clouds and purple smoke. Then wind cleared away all but the skeletal remains of the world.

Timkin, a surgeon in his old life, was one of the few who had the foresight to build a bunker. It was lined with two-by-four shelving that held necessities for survival: canned and freeze-dried goods, blankets, flashlights, and bottled water. He installed a generator and a sewer system. He hid in the bunker during the change, and he did not see daylight until the first knocks came at his vault-like door.

A family of three—father, mother, daughter—stood before the entrance. Wide eyes bulged out of their pale faces; pupils danced.

"Please take out our eyes," the father said. "We don't want to see what comes at nightfall. We will give you anything."

Timkin's face wrinkled when he first heard the request. He counseled the family, but he did not receive the answers he sought. Eventually, he gave in to their cries for help, and he accepted their offering of bread. In exchange, he did as they wished. He sent them back into the world, bleeding, but relieved.

When others learned of what he'd done, the knocks at the door continued. Timkin took what they offered; he wasn't picky. Food, medical supplies, and water were the usual. Other times it was simple items, such as lip balm or matchbooks.

Occasionally, Timkin bartered for items he needed to run the bunker, such as oil and gas for the generator. This ran the heater and the incandescent bulb that hung over the operation chair. It also ran the suction pump. Gravity took the eye tissue away.

Once, a boy brought fingernail clippers. Timkin initially refused the offering because he felt bad for the child, but the boy insisted.

"You never know when you might need to trim your nails," the boy said, innocently.

Timkin trimmed nine of his ten fingernails. The last—his index fingernail—he grew long and sharp, like a tusk. He used it to clean the eye sucker.

*

The knocks became less frequent after the first year passed. Timkin wondered how long he could live if they stopped showing up, especially after his last patient's offering.

"Hunnert pounds," the man with stark blue eyes said.

"Money is no longer good," Timkin said. "You must know that."

"Please," the man begged. "There's notin' left out there. The world's a scab. I don' wanna live like this no more. Take me eyes, so I can be free from what comes at night."

Timkin could not turn him down. "I will help," Timkin said.

"But, no one will tell me what lurks out there. Will you?"

"Hart to explain. We see only its shape. It comes from the woods. By the flickering light of our fires, we see it hobble towart us, makin' that gawdawful clicking sound."

"What is it?"

"Please take me eyes, please," was his only reply.

Timkin strapped him to an old, metal pilot's seat that served as the operation chair. He lowered the glowing bulb to just above the man's forehead, revealing tiny beads of sweat. He dipped his fingernail into rubbing alcohol, cleaned the mouth of the suction hoses with the fingernail edge, and then placed the gaskets over the man's eyes. He held the hoses firmly to the sockets and turned on the system.

Within a second, both eyes were plucked. Timkin watched the eyeballs make their way through the semi-transparent hosing—the pupils turning purple as they mixed with red socket fluids—to the PVC pipe that drained under the shelter. Then he removed the hoses, filled the man's sockets with gauze, and wrapped a handkerchief around his head to keep it all in place.

The screams lasted minutes, but they felt like an eternity. When the man caught his breath, he said, "Thank you."

*

After a month without patients, Timkin was emaciated and running out of water. He would have to try to survive out there.

Perhaps, everyone died, he thought. *Perhaps, what they did not want to see has eaten them. Perhaps*, it *has died.*

He cracked open the bunker door and peered up the long stairwell. The setting sun cast shadows on the steps in front of him. He climbed, one step at a time, breathing heavily from his weakened condition.

At the top of the stairs, he could see the sun dipping below the horizon. It was too late to explore. *It* would come soon, they had told him. He would wait for daylight.

As he turned, he caught a glimpse of a silhouette against the mountains, miles away. He paused and then saw movement. As darkness fell, it moved toward him. *Still plenty of time to turn back down the stairs.*

Curiosity held him a moment longer. It moved quickly now. It was getting closer.

As it neared, Timkin's face flushed, and his lips parted. He did not gasp, but he sucked in air. He had to breathe.

He could make out its shape, which seemed to change from gas-like to solid. It developed many legs.

Then the hobbling noise—*click clack click clack*—grew louder.

Timkin raised his arm, slowly, and brought his fingernail to his eye. He rested the tip above his eyelid.

Click clack click clack.

Just as a spiny leg came into a circle of remaining light outside the bunker, Timkin understood why everyone had sought him, and he raised his fingernail to his eye.

#

Michael Carter is a writer from the Western United States. He comes from an extended family of apple orchardists in Washington and homesteaders in Montana. He enjoys cast-iron cooking and wandering remote areas of the Rocky Mountains with his dog Hubbell, primarily along the banks of the Gallatin River. He's online at michaelcarter.ink and @mcmichaelcarter.

SHADOWS

"Nothing in the universe
can travel at the speed of light, they say,
forgetful of the shadow's speed."

– Howard Nemerov

I Need That Ride

by Amanda Chiado

Mike Tyson's hot air balloon is made of gold thread,

Cured spider silks from the rice fields of Indonesia.

The strands are harvested in late summer, which

Gives them their glint and floatability. Mikey did it

For his mother, did all of this for her. She wanted

To whip around the world, twice. She had bad knees

Though. Nothing you can do with rickety ol' knee caps.

That's how the streets get you, turn your moon pies

Into skipping stones. "Mama, the balloon is ready."

It was Thursday. The luckiest day of the week,

But her knees had turned to lead. She was stuck

Kneeling at her bedside near a velvet deity. "Come on

Mama." She couldn't rise. Mikey yanked her up, fueled

By champion blood, even wore his gilded belt for grace.

Every time he yanked he heard ripping, her body

Parting at it weaknesses. "Baby," she said, "the golden

Threads won't get me home." Just then, in a whoosh

She crumbled from the knees up and the knees down.

He lay in the ashes thinking of snow angels on Mt. Hamilton,

Scooped up the pile with big hands, sweet spilled sugar.

There was a horizon waiting. The great shimmering

Balloon swayed on his golf-course lawn and rose up

Against the horizon after he slumped into the basket.

His mother falling like bread crumbs from his pockets.

#

Amanda Chiado used to be a unicorn archaeologist, but now she takes up space as a doorbell mechanic. She's thinking about you and your tender eyes. Read more of her work at www.amandachiado.com.

Episode

by Fredric Koeppel

"... the consciousness that my guilt is beyond question."
Franz Kafka, *Diaries 1914 to 1923*

When a couple of punks in their cups
are beating the crap out of you in the alley
behind the bar, for no reason except their belief
in the process and a salute to camaraderie,
so no hard feelings, chum, you feel each thud
of a boot to your gut, each smack of the bat
to your face, as rebuking your life of thoughtless
illegitimacy. Not that this debacle is entirely
your fault—there's such a thing as being
in the wrong place at the wrong time, but we're
not looking for a handy definition of history
here. By the way, an Uber driver at the front door
wonders where the fuck you are, and if you
manage to crawl into the back seat of his car,
he may whisper to the rear view mirror:
You reek of fear and stink of joy. There's
plenty more where that came from, boy.

#

Fredric Koeppel is a former college English teacher and a longtime journalist (now freelance) in the areas of the arts, books and culture. He writes the wine review blog biggerthanyourhead.net. He lives in Memphis where he and his wife try to manage a pack of rescued dogs.

Lily 19

by Stuart Airey

You weren't what I ordered
but I took you in anyway
well it was 3am
you were obviously broken
the angle of your left arm
you headed straight to the window
looked out over the city
etched a perfect snowflake in the glass
it wasn't even winter

You watched me all night
I pretended to sleep
I think you smiled
that special way with static
moving the hairs on my neck
finally I dreamed a lake
when you didn't move
with the sunlight
I got up to make coffee

It was cute at first
you spoke French
but couldn't cook
or walk in heels

scrambled my passwords
set off car alarms
and those nights
you jumped off the balcony
made it up the 5 floors
before I got to the door
when no one was watching

When I dreamed you were rewiring me
I woke to find you were
some nanobot thing I guess
a delta of spreading slender tipped joy
by the time they crashed through the windows
we were fractal mirrors
our blood the sea of Nectar

We are the moon now
liquid without water
cruising the night vendors
our favourite Hungarian
I get the groceries
you smudge the bank accounts
we laugh at our quirks
my rib
your arm

#

Stuart Airey lives in Hamilton, New Zealand and wanders the labyrinths of his tortured mind, occasionally putting pen to paper. He was a finalist in the Sarah Broom Poetry Prize 2018 and has been published in the *Ocotillo Review*. He has performed several multimedia poetry evenings and is working on his breakthrough project.

If I Am Then I Must Be Now

by Andrew Romanelli

I would see him as remembrance of a later self
among the young mothers in privet-choked
waiting rooms—squares writing in circles,
absconding the blue lines of dime-store composition books,
scribbling contagious in the rose stare of conjunctivitis.

He would walk out with the intent to purchase air
in the newspaper-bestrewn, coffin-shaped courtyards,
while Betty Ford drifters in pigeoney car coats
strung along children in gold paper crowns,
humming forgotten cartoon songs coded in omniscience.

In a small globe our bitty dreams are shaken up.
You will feel so low that when you reach up,
you'll touch the bottom.

As kids we flexed whole ribs under faded, soft-spun
cotton tees that would billow out around us in a jaunt
from a Walgreens where packs of Blacks get glommed
and hawked to them lungers on Lake Mead Boulevard.

In that same stretch come sundown, when the *good people*
pushed dented, neurotic metal carts into bustling

grocery stores—we would hold up lines with loose,
crinkly, food stamp dollars—dirty faces drawn sad,
aiming down our own noses at empathy around.

I would steal books from bookstores, read them
then sell them to secondhand bookstores.

Now, I cover the emptiness with each of my fingers,
roll snake-eyes into the soft click of a rust-jacked wall.

There was promise in our textbooks and afternoon television,
cereal bowls full of puffy charms, soggy dreams...
They might as well be the green new vogue.
　　　　If we ever had anything at all, tell me about it in a joke.

#

Andrew Romanelli is a slot machine in a grocery store. A Holy Joe of
neologism. A cactus hugging flâneur of districts and no-go
neighborhoods.

How did you die

by Erin Kirsh

by accident, the first time
by design the next.
disease had its turn, and famine often.
they took my home
then the elements took me.
there was the time i was dragged
through town tied to a panicked
horse my last act to paint the dust
with blood and brain, memories spilled
like saloon whisky. there was the war, the bear
the hired hit, and the vehicle. the false start
where i never made it out
of the womb, nurtured
to death. twice i gave
up, once rightly, once not.
guns of various models
men of many stripes, the boat
carrying me to a new life
to safety met with a torpedo
with an iceberg with a captain
whose love for opium was greater
than his love of the job, a bomb
and a current rushing joyful
toward the sea. a cavity a scarcity

a revolution a mosquito a bee
and a swelling in my throat
a sandwich and a swelling
in my throat, old age a sweet
handful of times, though the age
kept aging through the ages, once
it was the 74th year that did the trick
that ferried me through the door
down the hall and into the next
foyer, what will kill me
in the end i think is when i've
collected time in every atrium, until
the bowl of my hands can't hold
more air.

#

Erin Kirsh is a writer and performer living in Vancouver. A Pushcart Prize nominee, her work has appeared or is forthcoming in in *The Molotov Cocktail*, *The Malahat Review*, *Cosmonauts Avenue*, *Maudlin House*, *EVENT*, *Arc Poetry Magazine*, *QWERTY*, *CV2*, *the /t3mz/ review*, and *Geist*, where she took second place in their postcard short story contest. Visit her at www.erinkirsh.com or follow her on Twitter @kirshwords.

My father, bored as a parrot

by Julia Webb

but with duller feathers,
pecks at the bars of his cage
and my fingers when I open the door
for an attempted rescue.
Fuck off, he squawks, *fuck off fuck off!*

My father, whose head blooms
like an exploded firework,
who excels in all his gunpowder colours,
can't come to the door because today
is his day for ironing his work trousers.
I put my mouth to the letterbox
to try and coax him out.
Come back next week, he shouts.

My father is caught in the matrix
of his mind, he spends days, weeks,
trying to find a way back out,
sometimes his screen goes inexplicably black,
sometimes his program freezes,
sometimes the only way to reach him
is to switch him on and off.

My father, the budget supermarket
likes his food organic
but prefers not to pay through the nose,
his aisles are strip lit and cluttered,
you can't always find what you need.

#

Julia Webb lives in Norwich, UK where she is a poetry editor for *Lighthouse* and works for Gatehouse Press. Her first collection, *Bird Sisters,* was published by Nine Arches Press in 2016 and her second collection, *Threat*, was published by Nine Arches in 2019.

The New Model

by Jennifer Lynn Krohn

Again, we woke up to a new mother.
Father, what happened to the old mother?

This one's better! A brand new model!
    Cutting edge!

The stranger served us dinner, put us to bed.
The next morning a new new woman woke us.

Each missing mother left behind clues:
    a black silk dress,
    a white tennis shoe,
    a cook book with copious notes,
    a half knitted sock,
    a butterfly knife,
    a book with a shirtless man on the cover.

We hid these mementos under our beds

next to our journals and girlie mags.

We wrote a list of names
but could never remember any of theirs.

We just called them mom.
We didn't ask them
        their favorite color.
        their favorite film.
        their favorite song.

    We didn't ask if they had brothers, sisters,
        parents of their own.

When we tried to file a missing persons' report,
the policeman called our house and said

I have your mother on the phone.

#

Jennifer Lynn Krohn writes stories that make her friends and family ask, "Are you okay?" She is okay and has published work in *The Golden Key*, *Coffin Bell*, and *Storm Cellar* among others.

Yard Sale

by Karen Mandell

Useless, I could tell instantly.
Baby toys in plastic orange and red, grimy fry pans,
bent hollowware burning in the sun.
I walk in past the woman and the baby sitting on the concrete
    stoop.
I'm on my way out before I see the books piled on the grass,
their pages soft with age, the damp dried out of them.
The Sun Also Rises, the striped Scribner edition.
Do I have this one at home?
I crouch down and turn limp pages, not reading, brushing off
    dust,
unwinding a tendril of cobwebs from my finger.
The odor of paper stored in boxes too long.
This one's not worth it, broken spine, even for a quarter.
I put fusty Hemingway down.
The baby cries, his voice quavering and scratchy.
The woman picks him up and says it's time for a nap,
you're ready aren't you, you'll lie down for a little while.

I stand up, the sun hot on my hair.
I want to lie down, a baby, in a darkened room with only a thin
     cover.
An opened window with a fan going somewhere.
I'd close my eyes even if I didn't really want to
because there's not much fight left in me right now.
The baby whimpers.
I forget what city I'm in,
whether it's Minneapolis or Boston before that or
Chicago back even further.
I'm a burnished nub, everything rubbed out of me,
clarified. Even so, I have to get back to the car,
do the things that make it go,
add on to myself the crumbled pieces
that fell off and lie there, in the grass.

#

Karen Mandell taught writing and literature at several colleges, high schools, and senior centers. She likes writing about everyday life and the details that can, hopefully, propel us to broader visions.

He Smelled Like Grass

by Amanda Chiado

When he fell from the Ferris wheel
I closed my eyes to think of kissing him.

My heart, a madness of gears oiled
by the scent of boys. God, how good

it would have felt. He did not open
his wings when he descended. Father,

They'd not grown in yet. I had a crush
on him, and his holy-light eyes. Cotton

candy-blue, fell as well. He'd bought it
with his own money. He smelled like grass

from mowing lawns for five dollar bills.
His reluctant mother let him go out alone.

He walked to the unhinged fair to meet me.
My father was bungee jumping, would

Not let me go to out alone, trigger-scared
Of skinny boys and their hot-heavy hands.

I was looking up when gravity waved hello.
My father on thread of elastic, the freed boy

Falling toward me, but landing harder
Than all the tempered angels had hoped.

#

Amanda Chiado used to be a unicorn archaeologist, but now she takes up space as doorbell mechanic. She's thinking about you and your tender eyes. Read more of her work at www.amandachiado.com.

Rebirth

by J V Birch

She'd not long been a cat when her mother
came home one day to find her torturing
a mouse and squeaked *enough is enough!*

And so she thought about what she could be,
though she'd miss the clean pink of her mouth.
A fish is out of the question. She could never

fathom water, all that depth makes her insides
out. A bird could work, but extreme heights send
her dizzy. Maybe a dog instead without being

mastered…a thin movement catches her
eye. Now a spider, that would be interesting,
something to panic the edges. She'd have fangs,

a presence in corners, hello the unsuspecting
with a smile like split clowns. She feels her legs

multiplying as her tail disappears, fur thinning

on the hulk of her, mouth becoming mandibles,
a lick of lightening at her ends. In her slick
new self she quickly scales a kitchen wall,

as her mother starts buzzing below

#

J V Birch lives in Adelaide. Her poems have been published in Australia,
the UK, Canada and the US. She has three chapbooks with Ginninderra
Press and a full-length collection, *more than here*.

LEGENDS

"Legend remains victorious
in spite of history."
– Sarah Bernhardt

The Night of the Last Dreams

by Donna L. Greenwood

They were talking about God when the first owl appeared. She asked her lover whether he believed in God. He smiled and said that God was a fairy tale told to the feeble-minded to make them feel better about their shit lives. They were camping in the woods, and after these words, they heard a rustling in the trees above them. It was sitting on a branch—white-feathered and moon-eyed. Expectant. Listening. The first owl. That night, as they made love, she felt its feathers on her face. She watched her lover's eyes grow hard and round. His teeth drew blood.

They began to dream of owls. In the mornings they would share their dreams, open-mouthed and smiling at the similarities. They kissed and believed their love was so strong that their minds had melded. Beneath the morning rays, there were fears—unspoken because they were unspeakable.

As swift as madness, the owls descended until each branch bowed with their weight. Their dark silhouettes carved feathered scars into the black sky. They sat motionless in the fumy mists that were wrapped around trees and homes.

People closed their curtains during the day. The owls stared at them through the glass and made them think of murder. Old men screamed in their beds. Some said it was because they were closer to death; some said it was because they understood more than their rational minds could handle. Their screams were maddening. She watched her lover's knuckles grow white; she watched his eyes darken.

On the night of the last dreams, the children disappeared. Their mothers clung onto empty playsuits, curling their fists around vapours, trying to rebuild their children from air. When she heard them curse God for taking their babies, she looked at the owls and whispered, *Don't. Don't speak about God.*

Without sleep, people wandered in the night. They mumbled prayers and curses and spells. The owls watched in silence as tempers frayed, hot and bloody. Bodies, beaten to a pulp, were left in the streets to atrophy.

Before he vanished, her lover told her that his dead mother had kissed him on the mouth. He said she visited him often, ever since the owls had appeared. Later, she awoke alone, holding onto a lock of his hair and the memory of sex, and she knew that it was not the owls who had taken him. She knew that it had never been about the owls. The owls acted only as a portent.

One by one, the lights blinked out and they stared at one another in the darkness. Sleep never came. As they sat alone in hidden corners, a terrible understanding iced its way through their brains. The good people burned their bibles, their korans, their grimoires; the bad people slaughtered other bad people. Priests hanged themselves in sycamore trees. Old women ate their cats.

It was said that you would hear them before they came for you. The noise was supposed to be loud, like a roaring engine, and then, it was said, you would see a bright, dazzling light. The owls were the first clue. One for sorrow, two for joy, three for eternal emptiness.

There were three owls perched outside her window. Three; her time had come. She waited for the inevitable roar. With her lover's hair cast between her fingers, she knitted herself a prayer. The White would descend soon. It took them all in the end. This was the only certainty now.

When they came for her, she knew them. She had always known them. As they reached for her, a white, planetary light fingered her body. She uttered the name of the only one who could save her from them.

'Oh God, help us.'

A long, grey body stood before her, and, although she could see no mouth nor find no face, she heard its words in her mind:

'We are God.'

And she knew that all hope was lost.

#

Donna L Greenwood lives in Lancashire, England. She writes weird flash fiction and short stories and occasionally tries to write the odd poem, with emphasis on the word 'odd'. You can find examples of her work in *The Airgonaut, Ellipsis Zine* and *The Corona Book of Ghost Stories.*

Their Soil Freshly Turned

By Chris Panatier

I get home and the wife says another waxwing suicided itself into the bay window and could I put it out with the others. They say that window reflections look like a continuation of the great outdoors to a bird. They just fly into them and BOOM. It's not like they suffer.

I do.

A little bit of me just tears apart when those little guys' lives blink out. One second singing and free, and the next deader than fried chicken.

I look at the latest. He's got nice, chestnut-brown wings fading to dusty black, with red stripes on the tips just like a commie general. A common tree bird to most—an exotic far as I'm concerned.

I carry him and a shovel out to our little grove. I know where not to dig because I mark each grave with a little piece of fence picket labeled with the date and a name. The waxwing will be Simon, probably 'cause I ain't got a Simon yet.

So I dig a hole and he gets a shroud of paper towels, since

Martha's put the kibosh on me using her fabric remnants. I lay a dandelion just so on his face and commit him to the earth.

When I'm done, I look over to where my lumber should be. It's disappeared, no doubt pilfered by the Snyder kids down the way—always coming in here trying to take what isn't theirs. Then again, I guess I'm no different, collecting scrap around town without much asking for it. There just seems a sense of ownership in the aggregation. Anyway, the most the Snyders ever took was a rusty tool or two. They got eyes on Darcy, my old '58 International—she's worth a mint, but she don't start, so good luck trying to pinch her.

With no wood about, Simon gets a little cairn of river rock.

Over the next weeks, things get busy. Maybe it's the fall setting in or the shifting wanderings of the regional fauna. One day, it's an opossum I named Tony, the next, a little racoon dubbed Bandit, because what else are you gonna name a racoon? I wonder over the cause of it, why they've chosen my yard as the place to exercise their mortality. Maybe word got out that I treat them well, so they figure to limp on over here before they give up the ghost.

By the end of November, the grove looks like an honest-to-God model train cemetery.

*

The grandfather in the downstairs hallway runs an hour slow and it's already chimed two, so I know it's past three when I hear the doors to the barn. Dollars to donuts it's the Snyder brats trying to boost Darcy again.

I head out, bypassing my rifle in favor of the Louisville on account of I know these kids. But when I get to the garage, I see right off it ain't the Snyders. I'll be goddamned, I say.

I don't register who knocks me to the ground or what with, and the blood in my ears is garbling voices. One of 'em boots me in the stomach and I'm swinging, but the bat's gone.

The guy's yelling about where are the keys, and before I can tell him that Darcy needs a fuel pump, my teeth are on the concrete. Now I've been hit before, and hard, but this guy brought the wood. For the first time in a long time, I'm starting to get worried. I try to holler but I'm walloped again. One tells another to go take care of the old man's wife.

Lights reflect off the slick of my blood. A trailer's backing in. Guess they aim to carry Darcy out. *So carry her.* I got to get to Martha.

And that's when I see Bandit. Crouched up near the front of the truck pushing the trailer, half his face is gone, one side of it just a skull with a tiny eyeball hanging out. I see others too. There's Tony, standing beside Grandma the wolfhound. On the trailer are the fat grey squirrels, Rudolf and Malcom, that I buried in late September. I see Charlotte the bobcat peaking around the corner, and Jeremiah the black snake hanging from the lathe. Hell, there's the ridgeback that croaked back in May. Shooting in from a crack in the wall come all fifteen of the Ratersons like a little worm-eaten varmint army.

None were in great shape when I gave them to the earth. They look worse now.

I reckon it's all got to be a hallucinatory delusion brought on by my cracked skull. But then the cooper's hawk I named Hawkins gets the lead guy in the neck and his jugular stream gets me full in the mouth. Can you taste a hallucination?

It's like a twister's hit with animals flying this way and that, dropping perps like potato sacks. The guy in the truck steps out with a twelve-gauge and starts throwing buckshot. Some hits Darcy. He stops firing and I figure he's spent his shells, but he turns and I see that his face is off. Nearby, a couple of deceased barn owls tussle with it like a dishrag.

The action stops and I'm breathless. Through the eye that ain't swollen shut, I count five limp bodies. The undead gather 'round. I figure they've saved me for last, but they just sit there. I point weakly to the house and speak my wife's name and they troop off.

Gunshots. A man screaming. I pass out.

*

The next morning it feels like I slept in a rock tumbler. I beg Martha for a sip of bourbon. She brings tea. Later on, she surprises me with a little pile of fabric cuttings and helps me limp down from the house. We kneel in the glade together, resetting the tiny headstones at the head of miniature graves, their soil freshly turned.

#

Chris lives in Dallas, Texas, with his wife, daughter, and a fluctuating herd of animals resembling dogs (one is almost certainly a goat). He writes, "plays" the drums, and draws album covers for metal bands. As a lawyer, he goes after companies that poison people. His short fiction has appeared in or is forthcoming from *Metaphorosis, The Molotov Cocktail, Ghost Parachute, The Ginger Collect, Tales to Terrify, Trembling with Fear, Ellipsis Zine, Defenestration* and others. *The Phlebotomist,* Chris's debut novel, comes out in September 2020 via Angry Robot. Plays himself on Twitter @chrisjpanatier.

What You Will and Won't Do
(About the Man in Your Garden)

by Joely Dutton

Nothing will terrify you like that eye contact. You'll be cleaning dishes at your kitchen sink, looking out at your garden and the flow of fields beyond it, when a large man will step into the frame from stage-right, inches from the window. You'll catch your own choked scream like a sound effect from a place you weren't aware of, and feel the burst of adrenaline spike through you as quick-spreading fractals. A man on your property. His eyes, and their intent; a message penetrating the thin pane and drilling your own eyes right through to the sockets. It will be the first nightmare you couldn't wake from, and it will make the frail civility of your life until that moment absurd.

It's the explanation you'll give for feeling out the carving knife at the bottom of the water and heading out there with it. For not waiting inside your house, the only one for miles around, and hoping help reaches you before he does. It's the reason you'll state for punching the blade through his sternum as he comes toward you. Him or you, *him or you*, any hesitation forfeits choice. Him or you. You'll choose him.

You'll dial 999 as the dishwater turns murky around abandoned pans and as the unknown man's body bleeds out on your decking, staining wooden panels. Your shaking index finger will transfer his blood onto your phone and you'll leave an impression of the square number 9 button in red on your right cheek as you listen to the ring tone. You'll tell the calm operator about the intruder, the one you think you might've killed and Oh God, you'll say, between sobs that come from so deep down you'll feel their vibration within your head. Things outside your head will become surreal. Your house like a cartoon drawing of the one you lived in earlier.

When they arrive, the police will pour you sweet tea. An officer will link your arm with hers and lead you to a different room while paramedics stretcher the man out through your front room. When you hear the ambulance start up again, you'll ask the police woman if he's alive. Or is he…? You won't be able to say the other word, though you'll know already that he is.

At the station, you'll ask the interviewing officer who the man was. You'll know that already, too. He was the kind-looking man you saw driving along the country lane near your house, the one you frantically waved down to the roadside and pleaded for help. The man you needed to drive your injured dog to the vet, because your car wouldn't start and your dog might die waiting for a taxi this far out of town. You led him through the back gate of your property, and asked him to wait there in your garden while you went to grab the small dog, who you said was wrapped in a blanket on your sofa where she'd been having seizures.

It was the man who looked confused when you came back outside without a pet, your hands concealed behind your waist. Who looked alarmed when he saw the knife, moving, a second too short to act so his hands only clutched yours on impact, too late to push them away.

The police will believe what you tell them. They'll find his car parked on the country lane. They'll suggest voyeurism, though no one will be able to prove the man's intent.

A judge will hear your statement and clear you of manslaughter charges on the grounds of self-defence. Of perceived risk. And you'll mentally scratch through the list you'd planned out, when each turning point goes the way you expected it to, until this score card ends and you win. You'll go back to your house in the countryside, free to start again. Like you knew you would.

You won't doubt that you can do it. You won't even twitch a smile when the sweet-tea officer tells you that, living alone in a remote area, it might be worth getting a dog.

#

Joely Dutton lives in Stafford where she gets startled by things through the kitchen window (usually a branch or a cat though). Say hello @JoelyDutton.

The Eyes

by Andrea DeAngelis

He only lets us out at night. We think it's a he, for father was always bigger than mother. Who we were before this endless cycle is decomposing, who any of our parents were, are only shrouds of thought. I can't remember them and they must be dust by now. We only live one night over and over again.

My favorite time is when he has not yet woken, when the light is dying and we aren't yet. That is when you might see us before the dusk slips away. At twilight, we run with the wild boars. Our shadows meld and splay in the greenish mist. Our pursuit gets us ready for him to hunt us.

I am older now than I remember, but I do not remember much except how he will kill us, slashing with a reaping hook as we run and fall. Our palms all scabs and scars. Hard and dark rusty globs under the surface, the damage never to completely heal, the raw and weeping skin growing translucent. I peel back my scabs, yellow-brown and crusty, to feel something again. Most of the jagged pieces peel away easily, only slightly catching around the outlines of my eternal wounds. If only I could wear another's flesh like him, I could get away. The wolf skin he wears flaps like wings as he chases us. Running and running, our lungs shrunken and gasping at the end of each night, when he always finds us.

Even so, it is beautiful here. I never appreciated the Sonian Forest when I was alive, when I could leave a mark that I exist, that this nightmare is only a nightmare and not my life. Sometimes we claw away at the bark, wanting to leave flesh behind as evidence, hoping someone will find us in this land of tall trees, fog and moonlight, mouths inside trunks, moss grafted onto skin, hollowing out, becoming desiccated again and again.

I don't remember how I got here but I know I will never leave. The night slits awake when his eyes open, those bloody irises and clots of black pupils will be the last thing we see in the glowing darkness. In those nameless hours, we die. He stares into us, boring into bone, while slashing, chopping and stabbing. Those eyes, great and large, fathomless. None of us has ever survived the whole night into dawn. I can still remember the sun, I want to feel it again.

Hell is recurring, that is how you tell it is hell. Sometimes there are only eight of us, other times eighty but there are never enough. He will never stop hunting us. You tell yourself that he is finished, satiated from gorging on all his killing, but the holes inside him only make him more ravenous.

The eyes will not die. He is the wolf he skinned alive. He doesn't need his hook to hurt me.

Which one of us will fall first tonight? Which one of us wants it over as quickly as possible? Prey that runs is usually chased. Prey that stands its ground may be able to bluff and stall the wolf. I've found my way to the deep river tonight, but he waits for me and I struggle against the current because I've never learned to swim. Is drowning worse than him breaking my spine? I will never find out because he will drag me out before I go under for one last icy time.

Peter, one of the older children (though we are children no more), after dozens of years, insists the hunter is a cacodemon. When Peter was living, he used to make up all sorts of tales and so we have trouble believing anything he says between wheezing and gasping for breath. He points out a dark red mass swirling under the skin of the hunter's broad back. But I wonder if it's the wolf's enlarged heart howling to escape. Peter says if we forgive him for killing then we will be free. But how can you forgive when you are being slaughtered? The agony only recedes when we are smashed into oblivion and the sky grays out.

Every night I see his eyes. I see them before me, behind me, to the right and the left and even inside me. You think you hear laughing, children laughing, but I haven't been a child for forty years. It is not laughter, it is mechanical and unbidden, it feels like metal teeth shredding. I used to love to run but now I'm raw with exertion, shaking and vomiting, dry heaving, breaking and crumbling into fallen leaves.

You believe in god but you overlook the devil. Your cars rarely stop for us and you shouldn't for he isn't done with his killing. He has killed us thousands of times and you could easily become his prey. It's happened before. As a driver swerves to miss our shadows fleeing across the road, he skids into the gray trees. The forest swallows the car and its passengers like a ripple contracting into the abyss. You shouldn't go near this ashen forest, you shouldn't get out of your car and walk into the fog, dizzy and stumbling. If you do, you will become lost and that is when he will stalk you and when he will have you.

Still, I wish you would hesitate, to witness our fixed looping existence. But you will throw your car in reverse. Time will then move forward for you. For us it is a cycle, a sickle of torture, endless and sharp. Wet ash by morning, coalescing from a single sprawling pool into individual phantoms, clots of darkening plasma, solidifying into limbs, flesh and fear, gathering ourselves to run and run. For though we are haunting, we are the haunted and always dying.

#

Andrea DeAngelis is at times a poet, writer, shutterbug, and musician (www.makarmusic.com) living in New York City. Despite her chronic insomnia, she can't seem to stay away from tentacles, claws, fangs and other dark folklore. Her writing has recently appeared in *The Molotov Cocktail* and *Timeless Tales*.

Extra Parts

by Rachel Sudbeck

Baylor's driving, because he's the one who saw her. He lives up the mountains anyway, so he's the one who's best at navigating those pinwheel turns, the sharp lefts that send Thompson and Connor sliding back and forth into me, stuck in the middle of the back seat.

These things are never as spooky as you want them to be. It's dark out, because you've got to go at night if you want to see ghosts, but it's just a regular dark, not misty or raining or anything in particular. Baylor's dad makes sure his kids' cars are in good working condition to drive them up and down the mountain for school every day, so it's humming smooth underneath us, and the headlights are doing a better than average job of illuminating the road. It's a sweaty spring night, and the air conditioning is churning away to compensate for the five sweating bodies packed into the car to see a ghost.

Baylor's got that Appalachian accent that makes some words twice as long and others half as short, so the story takes a strange rhythm when he tells it. He'd seen her around 6 a.m.;

he has to get up so early to make it to school on time. She'd just been there by the morning roadside, just for a second before another turn took her from Baylor's view, but it was clear as anything that she had three legs.

That's about the story's shape, the three-legged woman by the road, but it's one of those tales that has about eight different tellings. Mikey, who gets shotgun by default because he's so big, says she was a mother whose daughter got murdered and chopped up. She went looking for her daughter's body in the woods, but all she could find was a leg, which she held and cried over and wept over until it was all her ghost could remember to hold on to.

Thompson, on my left, says she was a girl who murdered her husband and sewed his leg to her thigh, though he doesn't seem to know why or how.

Connor, on my right, says he bets she has three tits too, and everybody laughs like it's so funny, even me.

Maybe I wish I had more friends who were girls, but only maybe. Other girls have started to terrify me. That morning I'd caught sight of Misty Thompson's naked back in the gym locker room and my whole body started to feel like it was steaming, like my pulse was sucker-punching my soul right out of my body. A group of girls were giggling in the corner and I felt like they were laughing at me, like they were seeing the naked me look at the naked Misty. I can't talk to girls any more than I can speak to the dead.

I tell the car, it's stupid, just somebody trying to spice up a boring ghost story by adding an extra leg. Baylor pulls over onto a shoulder, says this is where he saw her.

It's a steep stretch of road, so steep that the car is perched pointing up like a space shuttle. Through the windshield we can see a clear night sky, sparkling through the tree branches. We get out, stretch, stump around in the woods a little, but there's not anything. Connor does a whistle, calls out to the ghost girl like he would call out to a dog, makes smooching noises like he would for a cat, and I go back to wait by the car.

I'm sitting on the windshield looking through the branches, laced like cursive letters, when I see her, standing by the road like she's lost. Her hair is a bit of a mess, and I wouldn't call her dress old-fashioned, just old. The third leg coming out the back of her skirt looks pained and twisted, turned at the corners. It's part of her, she's not holding it, it wasn't sewn on, but it's not on her quite right. There's nothing scary about it.

Once, at a sleepover in middle school, Baylor and Mikey and I had waited in a closet to catch Connor's older sister changing. I told myself that they had talked me into it, but I wanted to see, because there was something about Sara that made me feel scared, in ways I did and didn't want to know.

We saw her, when she came in to get ready for her shower, slipped off her big army jacket and her sundress, slid the straps of her bra down her shoulders. Through the crack in the door, we could see. Her body was blooming with bruises, green and black and paler colors, down her back and the insides of her thighs. There were spots on that had been rubbed raw and bleeding. It was a hurt worse than I had ever seen.

When she left, we all of us ran from the room empty, not quite crying. We didn't say anything about it. Couldn't even breathe about it when Sara left home, the very second she was old enough to drive, and never came back. Nobody talked about her after. Their dad had thrown away all the pictures of her. Connor would mention her sometimes, but only sometimes. She wasn't even a haunting.

The three-legged girl's eyes are closed, her breaths come shallow. She was hurt and hurting once, and she still is.

I say something to her. I try to say it as gentle as I can. She looks at me, eyes open and wet in the dark. Her cheekbones are so sharp that I find myself thinking that they must be the first part of her face to burn in the summer.

When the boys come back, we pile into the car and drive back down the mountain, so steep it feels like we're falling. There's nothing in the car that I would call fear.

#

Rachel Sudbeck is your average queer who grew up in Nebraska and Kentucky equally; Southern people think she sounds very Midwestern, and Midwestern people think she sounds very Southern. Right now she's Getting Through It.

What Happened at Crimson Lake

by Erin Perry Willis

The Stories They Tell:
The lake eats children. Swallows them down into the dark deep; where a giant mouth filled with giant teeth gnaws forever at their bones. And there is a monster that lives in a cave at the bottom of the lake. It comes out at night, to feast on the leftover scraps, and clean the flesh from the giant teeth. Sometimes it leaves the water and ventures into town, stealing naughty children from their beds and feeding them to the lake, where their bodies are never found.

Once a woman drowned herself looking for her children. They found her three days too late, her hair tangled up in the reeds. If you listen closely you can still hear her calling.

For Your Part:
You always loved those stories. Once you went skinny dipping in the lake on a dare and won twenty bucks, which you used to buy lipstick and a push-up bra. You let your high school boyfriend take you there after prom, in his mother's

rickety old van, where you drank too much and struggled so hard that you threw up by the water in the same place we used to catch tadpoles when we were young.

You loved the lake. Its earthy, rotting-wood smell. Its buzzing insects. Its secrets.

The Stories They Tell:
The lake is cursed. Back in the old days, they used to hang witches from the trees, their bodies swinging, the crows feasting on their eyes. Then they burned what was left in a great pyre, and threw the bones in the water, where they took root in the mire. Sometimes you can still see the shards glistening under the surface, like schools of little white fish.

For Your Part:
When you were eight, you stole my Barbie dolls and buried them in the shallows by a large clump of poison ivy under the shadow of a rotting tree stump. You dug thirteen graves and popped each of their heads off before covering them with dirt and decorating each grave site with a marker made of twigs and grass. You gave them each their last rites, like the priest had done for our father, the last time we saw him in the hospital.

When I asked you if you'd seen the dolls, you told me that you didn't know where they had gone, but that you were sure they were in a better place.

I never did find their heads.

The Story He Told:
He said you had both been drinking. He said the whole thing was your idea. He said you'd begged him for it, had been begging him for weeks.

The Truth Is Slippery, Like An Eel:

Many years before we were born, an entire troop of Boy Scouts went missing out by the lake, their campsite abandoned. For five long days and nights, volunteers scoured the surrounding area, but found no trace or track in the mud and leaves. On the sixth day, they found the bodies: bobbing in the water, their faces unrecognizable, as if the lake had chewed them up and spat them out.

They buried all thirteen in a mass, unmarked grave in the local cemetery, though no one today can remember quite where, and there are families that still mourn, even though no one can remember even one of the thirteen names.

Once the lake was featured on the show Urban Legends. A psychic, a group of ghost hunters, and a camera crew tried to spend a night camped out on one of the lake's short, muddy beaches. They didn't make it to dawn. Hunted by mosquitoes, they abandoned their post, but not before they captured footage of thirteen bright red lights, flickering like fireflies, dancing on the water.

For Your Part:

You struggled so hard you threw up twice. Once on his tux, and once more after he left you there, your dress covered in mud.

For My Part:

I saw you, the night you decided you'd had enough. I heard you crawl out your bedroom window, and I followed you down to the lake, in my pajamas and rain boots, the trees leaving marks on my skin. I watched you emerge from your clothing like a white moth, your arms spread out wide, triumphant, like a witch cut loose from the choke of rope about her neck. And I saw you dive into the water, and when you didn't resurface, I followed you. I followed you in.

And what I found there was a door, shimmering like a prism. But what you found there, on the other side, I don't know, because it wouldn't let me in, no matter how hard I pounded, or how long I held my breath.

The Stories They Tell:

They don't call you a slut anymore, not after what happened, though I know they still think it. Instead, they call you That Poor Girl or simply That Girl, like they can't decide if you deserve their pity.

Sometimes they refer to you as The Drowned Girl. I actually kind of like that one. It reminds me of Hamlet's Ophelia.

For Your Part:

Though they searched for months, they never found your body, or any evidence at all that you'd been out by the lake the night you disappeared, except for the muddy nightgown you left discarded on the shore.

Our mother likes to believe you simply ran away, and that's true, in a sense.

Wherever you are, I hope it truly is a better place.

#

Erin Perry Willis is a writer and illustrator living in sunny southern California with her husband and two crazy (but adorable) cats. She loves dark chocolate and coffee, and if a genie offered her one wish, she'd ask for a personal chef. Find her on Twitter @Indigo_Summers.

The Man in the Green Hat

by Amanda Pollet

As often is true, it was the kids in town who spread the story first—the story of the unchanged man. He was real, or must have been, because even adults who considered themselves sane could recall seeing him—always in a queer green hat and often in a dull yellow suit. And as described by the collective, he remains mystically unchanged throughout history. The story of this man is exactly the kind that lends itself to add-ons and speculations. So this version has the flavor of the whole town and all its fears and wonderings. In this way, the man in the green hat *is* the town.

When the man was a baby, he was forgotten by his mother at a quilting convention where she took home her first quilt and forgot her first child. Some say she was killed by a swarm of angry red-winged blackbirds before returning to him, but most say she simply liked raising quilts more than raising babies. The man (then babe) was found by a stranger, who mistakenly asked a visiting pharmacist, "Is this your child?"

And the pharmacist, who was the sort who thought it might

be fun to raise a boy said, "Why yes it is," and it wasn't a lie thenceforth.

This pharmacist had many curiosities and scientific revelings. He also had a large house in the countryside with fifteen rooms (and fireplaces in all but three).

The pharmacist (naturally) was desirous to prolong the life of individuals. His concoctions cured ailments and extended old age, and his work was sought out and applied by prominent physicians. But what many did not know of was his unconquerable obsession to eliminate death altogether.

In his lab and library were stores of research and experiments with everything from lore about the Fountain of Youth to ancient recipes for potions giving eternal life. (Few that tell the story inform why the pharmacist would want eternal life when it would essentially put him out of a job, but listeners with a good imagination can enjoy a plethora of possible histories that make perfect sense of his psychological situation).

However, this is not the pharmacist's story being told.

This is the story of the man in the green hat who was being raised by the pharmacist who was struck with an idea the first night he took the boy home.

"What if," he said out loud to himself while staring at burning coals in the late evening (as he was the sort to do), "What if this boy never learns of death? What if he grows up never knowing death exists?"

It would be hard to pull off, he admitted. Almost impossible. But what interesting observations he could make while trying.

And so the experiment began. The staff of the house agreed to this concealment, and being paid such generous wages, they had no right to complain—even though it made liars of them all.

"What happened to Fido?"

"He ran away."

"What is that fly on the windowsill doing?"

"It's sleeping."

"Why do plants go away before winter?"

This one stumped the groundskeeper, who after some careful thought replied, "They're more clever than us and leave for the winter," which surprisingly prompted no further questions.

Most things, in fact, the boy accepted easily. He (fortunate to the experiment) possessed the opposite nature of his inquisitive father. One subject that seemed to be the exception to his typical indifference was that of aging. Any answer given to "Why do people get old?" was unsatisfactory. But the boy disliked being puzzled, so he grew to evade his own questions.

Perhaps he sensed that there was a very troubling reality lying just outside his realm of understanding that had best be avoided. Or maybe he had a dull, tiny brain. Either way, the non-curious boy eventually grew into non-curious man.

And as things are generally understood, there comes a time in adulthood when humans stop developing and begin to degenerate. It is said that when the boy reached this point in time, it became impossible for him to comprehend death. His brain fully matured, and if death was presented to him his psyche would reject it as unreality.

But what not even the pharmacist predicted is that not only the boy's mind rejected death, but also his body. He stopped growing, but never began degenerating. Some even say that he no longer needs to eat or drink, but most say that's utter nonsense—of course he needs to eat.

Our pharmacist, though, grew old and discovered an incurable cancer in his body. He could barely relay this information to himself, let alone the boy who was now a man (whose lack of mental acquisitiveness had begun to greatly disturb the pharmacist), and so one day he announced to the man that he was leaving. Any trouble that the man might have felt over this sudden declaration was outweighed by relief that he would no longer have to behold the sight of the aging, saggy body of his adoptive father (which had begun to greatly disturb him).

After the pharmacist left, so did the money, and so did the servants. The man in the green hat now lives all alone and has for a very, very long time. He is no longer protected from everyday occurrences in which living things meet their demise, but he simply does not apperceive them.

The pharmacist really did leave, and unable to cure his own death, he succumbed to it alone. His highest ambitions were realized, at least in one experiment, and so maybe this story really is his after all. But it is the sighting of the man in the green hat who inspires the telling.

For whether spotted by the young or old—no matter when the sighting took place—when the man in the green hat comes to town, he is the same. He does not age and he does not change. He comes about and leaves, avoiding the ending of anything.

#

Amanda Pollet is a Detroit-dwelling pre-school teacher who dabbles in outlandish and whimsical writing and cartooning as an outlet for creative expression and meaning-making.

Magdalene

by Maura Yzmore

After Father broke my arm for the second time in the first grade, Grandma said it couldn't be helped. I was just born unlucky, on the thirteenth, to a mother of whom no one spoke.

I tried hard not to tempt fate. Grandma taught me to stay away from ladders, black cats, and mirrors. To not step on cracks in the pavement. To hide in the closet or the attic or the next-door neighbor's when Father was about to come home from a triple shift, the third spent knocking back drinks at a bar two blocks away.

My luck improved as I got older and learned the rhythm of Father's comings and goings, my sight and hearing finely attuned to the slight changes in the pitch of his voice, the flare of his nostrils, the angle at which his caterpillar brow dipped toward his nose, all heralds that my luck would run out unless I made myself scarce.

But there was only so much good fortune in the world. The luckier I became, the worse it was for Grandma, her face purple and green where her son's meaty paws had landed, a color-coded calendar of my timely escapes—until the day she died.

I felt rage, so much rage toward the happy kids at my school and all the good luck they took for granted. So I helped relieve them of some of that abundant, decadent fortune; I helped them fall and scrape their knees, lose lunch money and homework, step on cracks in the pavement and bloody their noses.

But not Magdalene.

Magdalene, with thin, blue veins under translucent skin, her hair and eyelashes so blonde they were white. I tried to trip her up, get her to rip her dress, break her compact mirror, but she was always perfectly fine. She knew what I was up to, yet she smiled at me anyway with a warmth I'd known from no one but Grandma, and that made my insides burn and my eyes well up, and I couldn't tell if I was sad or angry or something else I couldn't name, and amid the helplessness and confusion I decided I would have some of Magdalene's good fortune if it was the last thing I ever did.

So I followed her home, keeping my distance. Each day, I'd follow her a bit further, until shame overwhelmed me and I went back home. I watched her walk under ladders and step on cracks in the pavement, carefree, as if none of that mattered.

The day a black cat crossed her path, I stopped, certain she would change her route. But Magdalene squatted, picked up the cat, then turned around and said to me, "We're almost at my place. Don't leave now." We walked side by side the rest of the way, the black cat relaxed in the girl's arms.

Magdalene lived in a small one-story house that backed into a wooded area. "Mom's not home yet," she said as she put the cat down and unlocked the door. The air inside was stale. Several cats, a bird, a fishbowl. Dozens of pictures of a smiling little Magdalene and a white-haired woman who looked just like her.

We went to the kitchen in the back. I asked for a glass of

water and drank it up in loud, desperate gulps.

"Thanks. I should get going..."

"Not yet," said Magdalene. "I've got something for you, but you have to help me get it. It won't take long."

We went out the back door and through the uncut grass to where the yard opened into the woods. Magdalene knelt on the ground by a tree, one of the roots sticking out like a giant knuckle. She plunged her arm into a hole beneath the root and pulled out a gray rabbit. She held it by the fur on the back of its neck like she'd done it countless times before.

As we made our way back, I noticed two metal rods, side by side, inches long and inches apart, sticking out of the house wall. Magdalene slid the rabbit's neck in between the rods, like on rails, then grabbed the animal's hind legs and yanked them up high, far above where the rods tethered the head.

I froze.

The rabbit's body went limp, its neck broken. It was over.

Magdalene seemed unmoved. I followed her inside, even though I couldn't really feel my legs. She placed the rabbit on the counter, pulled out a cleaver from a drawer, and cut off a hind foot.

"For you," she said, holding the rabbit's foot between her fingers for me to see. "It'll bring you good luck. But I need a few days to prepare and dry it."

My voice came back as a whisper. "Are, are you gonna make one for yourself?"

Magdalene shook her head. "No. A rabbit's foot is only lucky if it's received as a gift. I already have one, anyway." She took out a rabbit-foot keychain from her pocket. "Mom made this one for me."

I ran fingers through my hair. My hand was shaking.

"Magdalene...I...This is a lot to take in."

She smiled. "I know." She put the keychain back in her pocket, and the bloody rabbit foot right next to where it was severed.

I nodded toward the carcass. "What about the rest of it?"

"Dinner," said Magdalene. "My mom can butcher anything. She always says, 'We make our own food and we make our own luck.' "

Magdalene's eyes met mine.

"You know what else my mom says?"

I shook my head no.

"She says that any animal can be killed. No matter how big, mean, or scary. No matter who they are."

I swallowed hard. My face burned under Magdalene's gaze.

She stood up on her toes and placed a kiss on my cheek. "You're gonna love your new rabbit foot. And I know just how we can test it."

#

Maura Yzmore is a writer and scientist based in the American Midwest. Her fiction has appeared in *The Arcanist, Kanstellation, Aphotic Realm,* and elsewhere. Website: maurayzmore.com. Twitter: @MauraYzmore.

La Puerta

by Mark Purnell

Jim walked over to the corner bistro late in the day. The hot sun beat down on his white peasant shirt as he made his way to the outdoor bar overlooking a pale blue sea. His hair had grown too long the past few months as he focused intensely on writing poetry in his small bungalow. He'd resolved to cut it, but hadn't made the effort yet. Today, like every day, he needed some whiskey to fortify himself before a night of writing.

It had become one of his sacred rituals. Every afternoon, he would hang at his favorite bar, La Puerta, in the company of his friends and the ever-entertaining bartender, Olivierio. Get himself nicely lubricated while the sun set a deep red. Have a wonderful meal of black beans and rice with some form of protein. Sometimes he'd stay deep into the night for a fun round of off-key drunk karaoke, but would never sing. Over the years, they had all tried to get him up there, offering him the mic on many occasions, but the only thing he'd ever do is dance, drink and eat. Said he had a tin ear and nobody wanted to hear him carry a tune.

Sometimes, when the mood gripped him, he'd recite a poem or two, but only when he was the most drunk and then his voice would dramatically change octave or tone. Everyone assumed it was because he was *borracho* or being funny, which he seemed to have a real talent for. Under the warm light of the outdoor deck, with a mic in his hand, his hair hanging down over his handsome but aged face, he seemed like someone larger than life. No one could put their finger on it. But then, as soon as he was done reading, he'd stumble off the stage, bid his feast of friends good night and retreat to his "writing hut."

Jim loved the friends he had gathered on the small, thin raft of an island far from the glaring spotlight of L.A. He thought of them as he wandered home over the sandy shore, a mythical figure departing into the night. For some reason, reading his poetry and performing a little bit tonight had made him melancholy. For the first time in a long while, he missed his former life. The many women he had loved and who had loved him back a hundred times more. The adoring fans and his band of brothers who broke on through the doors of perception on many a transcendental night.

He had had a good world, more than enough to base a movie on. He had lived out all his fantasies and scaled the strangest of heights, but as he stepped up to the humble hut just off the white sandy beach, it was as if he were back on Trip's rooftop, homeless and staring into the vastness of the night. Penning his every thought and inner feeling as he swam to the moon. Trying to make sense of Jung and the will to power, while learning how to move a crowd of people, how to influence them and trigger a mass psychosis. He wanted to journey as deep into the cerebral and unknown as one could go, a musical psychologist and subconscious explorer, and tonight, sitting at his typewriter a little unsteadily, he would go there again and again as he explored his thoughts in rhyme and meter.

His journey had started on a beach after all, one sunny day in L.A., Ray and him just riffing ideas off each other like dime store cowboys, both surprised that what came out of Jim's mouth was pure gold. They climbed through the tide after that day, penetrated the evening that the city slept to hide. And what a majestic climb it had been. Sacred, profound and serpentine.

But then it all became too much, a chore. His health wasn't great after years of heavy drinking and people just wanted the same thing from him over and over again. To show his meat and act the fool. And so having outgrown his role as the ultimate rock star there was only one thing to do, disappear.

The small island where La Puerta was situated could only be reached by pontoon plane, and was only known to locals. Locals he had met on one of his many strange trips. They welcomed him easily, despite his meager Spanish speaking skills, because they saw a man in need of shelter, a rider on the storm in need of a port. They never bothered him, unless he was out and about at La Puerta or the local market shopping for groceries and beer. He was grateful for their acceptance and friendship.

It had all begun at the beach and it would end there too. He had fewer and fewer visitors from afar these days. Pam passed away a few years ago. Ray too. Robby and John were still around, but not up to travelling much, which was fine by Jim. He had his Crystal Ship, his anonymity, and with time his strange and fruitful days would pass too. A legend would return to the earth the way he wanted to. Untethered, unbothered and free. No one was going to throw his meat up on a screen or stage ever again. He had broken through and broken away.

#

Mark Purnell is a writer, investor and musician living in New York City. His writing has recently appeared in *The Molotov Cocktail* and he is currently working on his debut novel. Mark sings, writes and plays piano in the indie rock band MAKAR (www.makarmusic.com), who are in the midst of recording their third album, *Fancy Hercules*.

Revenge of the Ponderosas

by Michael Carter

Pa lost his job when they shut down the corporate sawmill over the spotted owl and clearcut. We had no idea, in the end, we'd also lose Pa.

Lumber was the only way he knew to make a living, so he opened his own mill. He hired some locals who were also out of work, and they made two-by-fours and strand board from the Ponderosa Pines that blanketed the land we called home.

Some folks were not happy. The owl and clearcut were all over the news, and the enviros and Nimbys were suing like crazy. But that didn't stop Pa.

"Nothin's gonna keep me from choppin' trees, 'specially some little birdie that might not even exist. Never seen one myself. Been in these woods my whole life. How's people s'posed to eat, anyway?"

The mill ran smooth thanks to Bryan, Pa's friend with a girthy neck that formed lines in the back of his head. Bryan promptly escorted troublemakers off mill grounds. Turned out, however, protesters were the least of our worries.

*

I noticed the first sapling while I was heading to school. While backing out of the garage, I saw a tree had sprouted smack in the middle of our gravel driveway. It was a few feet high, and I wondered how I'd overlooked it before.

There were more trees when I returned home. Pa had cleared an acre around the house when he built it to allow light and keep it warm in winter. About a dozen saplings now dotted the area surrounding the house.

"Looks like we got a weed problem," Pa said that evening. "Why don't you and your brother git the shears and chop 'em down?"

So we did. It was refreshing being outside, breathing the clean air, and Timmy and I felt as if we accomplished something besides homework and our usual chores. But, when I went to bed that night, I had a feeling they'd be back.

Sure enough, when I woke, about fifty trees twice as tall as Ma were up against the house and in front of the windows, like bars.

"Pa said you and Timmy have to trim back the weeds before heading to school, and if they're too thick, to get the hatchets from the shed."

"They're trees, Ma."

"That's what he's callin' them, so that's what I'm callin' them. Now get out there and cut."

So we did. I used a hatchet, and Timmy used a limber saw. It took longer than we thought, and we were both late for our last day of school before summer break. Ma excused our tardies saying a mudslide had blocked our access road.

After school, I saw Pa's truck out front. He was home early from the mill, and I wasn't surprised why. He was clearing a path through a barrier of trees with a chainsaw so we could get into the driveway and the front door. The trunks were thicker than Bryan's neck.

*

I woke every day that next week to Pa's chainsaw. He started it earlier each morning.

"Damn trees!" he'd yell when the blade stuck in a trunk. "I don't care how many rings ya got, I'm turning you to paper if you don't leave us alone," he'd say with a sinister chuckle.

We all rose before sunup the following week to help. We trimmed and hacked and sawed each morning. Eventually, we couldn't keep up.

Branches snapped the phone line, but we still had power from the generator. Ma cooked canned food from the fallout shelter that Pa had built in the cellar.

The trees engulfed the house such that it was pitch black during the day if we turned off the lights. We were running low on supplies, and Pa was running out of ideas.

"We could burn our way out," Pa said while flicking a Zippo inches from his nose, staring at it cross-eyed. "But most of these shitin' trees is too young and sappy. They'll just smoke."

"Good," I said, "the fire department will rescue us."

Pa glared at me. "Yer not makin' any sense. Never had nobody help me my whole life. I got this."

*

Pa jabbered during dinner, and when we played Skip-Bo to pass the time. He'd play a hand and then mumble nonsense. "Sure wish I could git into the boat-buildin' business and make some hulls with all these trees."

We became gaunt from the lack of food, and Pa worried us more each day. The walls, he said, spoke to him, and he hated them as much as the trees.

One day, a pine bough broke through the kitchen window. Pa jumped out of his chair, ran to the garage and grabbed the chainsaws. He handed us each one and said, "Help me!"

He yanked the pull cord, delivering blue-white exhaust

through the foyer. He took the chainsaw to the walls, making slash marks throughout the house. He sawed up our table, cabinets, and kitchen island. He went to the stairway and started into the railing.

"Where does it all end?" he yelled as his breath and sawdust filled the house.

We knew there was only one answer to Pa's question.

We came up behind him while he was working on the railing. He'd saw through the top of a railing spindle, kick it down, saw through the next, kick it down, while we closed in on him. He couldn't hear our saws over his own, or maybe he pretended not to.

With tears in our eyes, we took our chainsaws to Pa. He slumped to his knees while we tore into him; he never even looked back.

When he was finished, a breeze passed in the house. The first rays of daylight we'd seen in months splayed through the windows. Then, after we flicked our kill switches and the blades came to a stop, we heard the hooting of owls.

#

Michael Carter is a writer from the Western United States. He comes from an extended family of apple orchardists in Washington and homesteaders in Montana. He enjoys cast-iron cooking and wandering remote areas of the Rocky Mountains with his dog Hubbell, primarily along the banks of the Gallatin River. He's online at michaelcarter.ink and @mcmichaelcarter.

WILD

"Nature is relentless
and unchangeable."
– Galileo Galilei

Seasons in the Boneyard

by Andrew Bourelle

Part 1: Fall

The bull elk was tired from fighting and fucking. He led his harem high into the mountains, away from the bugling of his competitors, and found a wide valley full of wild grasses. The twenty cows and some of their children fed on the grasses, slept, and fed more. There was only one other bull in the group. A yearling, he, like the other young, would stay close to his mother until spring when she and the other cows would have new babies. He had a short set of antlers, barely more than nubs. He watched the bull, who wasn't his father, and tried to learn from the older male.

The food was ample. When the first snowfall came, the elk thought nothing of it. Instinct told them that they had time before they needed to descend into the lower elevations. When the second and third snows came, the cows began to feel nervous. But the mature bull made no effort to move, and the cows were unsure if they should strike out on their own. The bull stunk of his own piss and was sore from fighting, and all he wanted to do was eat and heal and come out of the crazy fog that had overtaken his brain during the rut.

As the snows came, the elk were able to trample drifts down in a vast swath and continue eating the grass underneath. But the snow outside of their feeding area grew higher, and soon they found themselves surrounded on all sides by a steep wall of white. The bull tried to fight his way out but the snow was too deep. He retreated back into the meadow, having finally faced a challenger he could not overtake. The elk were trapped in a bowl, with no way out and a dwindling supply inside.

The snow continued to fall.

Part 2: Winter

The bull elk shed his antlers, as did the young male. The cows nosed through the shallow snow to pick at what grasses were left. They chewed the bark from the few trees around them. They were able to keep the snow in their basin trampled down, but the walls grew higher and higher as the storms came almost daily. Their bodies began to thin, and, because they were starving, their coats refused to thicken.

The bull elk, weakened from the rut, was one of the first to die. He lay down in the snow and closed his eyes without ceremony. Snow drifted against his frozen fur. Two days later, the young bull's mother went to sleep and never woke. The young bull lay beside her and nudged her with his nose and tried to lick the ice off her fur as she had once licked the afterbirth from his.

The young bull thought about giving up, but there was a primal determination in him that made him fight. He and the remaining cows pushed their noses into the snow, searching for blades of grass. Their snouts were raw and bloody, their mouths full of sores. Ribs were visible, stomachs shrunken. The cows perished one after another, the fetuses inside staying alive briefly afterward in their warm placental sacks.

Then the unborn animals froze solid.

Part 3: Spring

One morning, the young bull awoke to find that none of the cows were standing. The sun was shining. The ground under his hooves was muddy with snowmelt. The bodies of the other elk were starting to stink. The bull approached the wall of snow and discovered that it wasn't as tall as he remembered. He tested the snowbank and found it soft. He scrambled up the slope and into the snow. He fought his way through the slush and disappeared down the mountain.

As the days warmed, flies appeared, buzzing around the bodies as they planted crops of maggots. Wolves were next, howling at their discovery. They ripped the rotting meat from the carcasses, snapped bones with their powerful jaws. Their spring shedding began, and tufts of wolf fur drifted among the bones like pollen. Birds came from the sky and pecked at the sunken yolks filling the eye sockets. Coyotes yipped as they ate the carrion and scattered the bones. A black bear feasted for two days. Later, raccoons and weasels and skunks came to pick the bones clean. Rivulets of water ran around the remains, and green stalks of grass grew up through the rib cages.

Part 4: Summer

Two humans—one male and one female—hiked high into the mountains, far from any trail, and came to a peak where they could see for miles. Clouds sailed below them, casting shadows like giant whales swimming through an invisible ocean. They ate sandwiches and drank from water bladders. They rutted sitting upright on a wedge of granite, kissing each other and declaring their love while trying to make a baby.

Hiking down, they came upon a skeleton, its bones bleached from the sun. They spotted more remains hidden in the tall grass. Most of the skeletons were not whole. Legs had been dragged away. Skulls were missing. But every few feet, they found a pelvis or a block of vertebrae or a jawbone still holding onto its teeth.

"Let's get out of here," the woman said.

They quickened their pace but stopped. A bull elk stood in the grass fifty feet away, looking around among the ribcages, white islands in a sea of green. His velvet rack was small, three or four points on each side. Maybe it was their imagination, but the bull looked sad. Mournful. He didn't graze. He simply stared at the meadow around him.

#

Andrew Bourelle is the author of the novel *Heavy Metal*. His short stories have been published widely in journals and anthologies, including *The Best American Mystery Stories*, *E Is for Evil*, *Pulp Adventures*, *Swords & Steam Short Stories*, and *Weirdbook Magazine*. Follow him on Twitter at @AndrewBourelle.

Ten Green Bottles

by Jan Kaneen

It's everywhere tonight. In the murmur of the trees and the hush of the wind, in the plainsong hum of my brothers and sisters as they make me clean, in the very flesh and bones of me. Strange to think it started as a lullaby. In Cork City, in that dingy bedsit above O'Reilly's bar.

Me and Mammy were all alone back then. She used to sing it to me soft and low, and when she'd finished and I still couldn't get to sleep, she'd say, now don't you worry my wee sweetheart nor be frightened neither, just keep on with the singing and I'll be back before you know it. Then she'd tuck my blanket up under my chin and go to the mirror and paint her lips scarlet.

And when she was gone, that's just what I did, sang it under my breath like a rosary or a penance, again and again to conjure my mammy back. And when the faded roses on the wallpaper changed into scary faces, I'd look at the real green bottles lined up empty against the wall, shining green and gold in the neon bar-light outside the dirty window, and I'd keep on singing.

It changed into a lament the night she didn't come back. I wailed it for days. And when they buried her body and sent me to live in the mud of Banteer with my Mammy's mammy, it changed again. Into a mantra. There was nothing could touch me with that mantra inside my head, not the jibes of the school kids when they called me Dirty Murphy, nor Sister Bernadette's pity when she saw the bruises; not even the sting of my grand-mammy's piety, waspish as it was.

I was sixteen when it changed again.

That June was the hottest ever and heavy with the flies. Swathes of them covered the sheep field and droves of them came into Grand-mammy's kitchen circling slow, making her almost mad. She swore and swiped, shouting *feckers* and *hoors*—but they rode the air and dodged her harm and I was glad that something could.

The spray worked better. She bought it in McGinty's Wholesale and shot peppery plumes of it up to the ceiling. I watched as they bounced off the whitewashed walls and flagstone floors, fizzing and buzzing metallic green as they whirligigged themselves to death. Grand-mammy looked nearly pleased as she crunched over them on her way out to feed the chickens.

'You know where the dustpan is,' she barked, closing the door.

They were still and dry when I swept them up, but out in the stink of the dustbin I caught a movement—an emerald abdomen shining gold, and gauzy wings glinting back to life. It rose up into the air, one greenbottle hanging in my eyeline. My heart raced with the strangeness of it and the low hum of its wings caught the mantra that was rolling around my head. I felt a flicker of something like recognition.

Grand-mammy's stick took me by surprise; knocked me clean off my feet.

'In the name of the saints,' she screamed, 'Are you singing to a filthy shit-crawler?'

She raised her stick again and the air moved. Gathering above her was a great swarm, glittering and green, a great sheet of pulsating light, droning, humming, buzzing. She followed my gaze and her face twisted as she turned her stick upon them, slicing fast and frenzied. But they split and lifted just out of her reach. And still she swiped, carving the air again and again until she was breathless. She bent over to catch a second wind, and they shoaled lower like a single thing, their music loud and low, then quiet, before they dropped, as a blanket might, over her head and hair and skin and clothes until she looked like something new—a shimmering green ghost made entirely from flies.

They must've sensed her heart stopping because they rose before she fell, hovering in the heat for a few long seconds, ordinary again, humming quiet like ordinary flies, then scattering—green smithereens shooting away, and in a second it was as if they were never there at all.

She was dead by the time she hit the floor, I'm sure of it. I tried to tell the Pruntys as I ran breathless into their yard. I tried to tell Father James too, and the Sisters when they came to make the arrangements. But they shook their heads and said I was in shock, which was no wonder at all what with the terrible heat and the biblical swarms and seeing my poor grand-mammy drop dead right in front of my eyes.

But that was a lifetime ago, a good lifetime I like to think. Two years at boarding school is a time best forgot, but I've been content enough scratching out a living here in the mud of Banteer. And I made it my business to learn all I could about *Lucilia sericata* and how they recycle the dead, but even when the internet came along, the entire digital knowledge of the human species couldn't explain what happened to my grand-mammy.

Only now, right at the end, do I start to understand.

What the living can't know about greenbottles is that they absorb everything.

Everything.

Ironic to think that when someone finds me here, they'll think I died alone—when the echo of Mammy's love is still humming in the heart of the swarm. Grand-mammy's too, even after seventy years. Less god-fearing and not so judgmental, but it's definitely her, inside them, inside me, inside us, and we are legion.

It's changed again now—into my requiem, I suppose, soft and low, echoing in the murmur of the trees and the hush of the wind, in the plainsong hum of my brothers and sisters as they make me clean, in the very flesh and bones of me.

#

Jan Kaneen lives below sea level in the manmade drained flatness that is the Cambridgeshire fens where she worries about climate change and rising water, and writes stories full of impotent grief.

Huntress

by Alpheus Williams

Mother is beautiful. Men look upon her and walk into lampposts, walls, and parked cars. Some walk into holes and vanish. A lorry driver, smitten with her appearance, veers into a tavern. The lorry explodes into flames, takes the tavern and folks inside with it. A huge funeral follows. People are upset. They want to torch our house.

Some are moved to resentment, some to envy, others to adulation. The constabulary sends a blind policewoman to plea with her to stay indoors, but when my mother speaks, the constable, overwhelmed with the music of her voice, resigns from the constabulary, learns the violin and travels the world. People line up for miles to hear her play, there is a sweet sadness in her music, lamenting that the blind will never gaze upon my mother's face.

The village butcher hangs himself in our tree, white pants and shirt, spotless black and white striped apron, tongue purple and swollen, a bloated slug, eyes bloodshot, wide and bulging. The tree festooned with fluttering leaves of amber, bronze, red, and orange that fall and tumble across our yard, the butcher swings from the tree to the rhythm of creaking branches. Gruesome, horrific, lyrical, moving.

It's because Mother no longer buys meat from him. She says she can't abide flesh that tastes of suffering. The butcher pleads innocence. He had no idea, he says. The beasts are delivered skinned and ready for sectioning. He looks no further. To his knowledgeable eye, the meat passes muster. It's grade A, has been checked and passed by health inspectors. All is in order.

Except it isn't, says my mother, she can feel their fates, their lives in pens, trapped in wire, food, and shit. Livestock up to their chests in dung, heads forced in troughs, destined to a fate of eating and shitting until a bolt blasts through their skulls and they are hanged, gutted, and skinned. She feels the horror of their living and the terror of their passing. Sorry, she can no longer patronise his shop. Bereft, the butcher closes his butchery, torches his house, purchases a fine new rope, dresses in his best. You know the rest. Villagers shake their heads. Fear and curse my mother. The fault of tragedy is laid at her door.

After the butcher, my mother raises chickens. Our breakfast eggs taste of sunshine and happiness. When chickens die, they die in my mother's arms, cradled like babies, a razor across their necks, so swift and gentle, the chickens close their eyes, swoon and slip away softer than dreams in feathery down.

She walks in gardens, vegetables and fruits lean towards her pleading to be plucked, flowers brighten, birds erupt in song. Under a full moon, my mother, archer and hunter, leads me into woods, dense, dark, and leafy. We stalk in shadows, peer into pools of light. A deer, soft-eyed and graceful, delicate as slow dance, meanders into moonlight. Mother pulls the bow, the fletching kisses her cheek. Eyes on target, she releases the shaft. A whisper thuds into a beating heart. The deer drops, knowing nothing other than wildernesses and freedom. We feast on venison.

Some say she is a wild thing. I reckon it's true. They say she is descended from the moon, a child of the virgin hunter Artemis, but I know there's no science in virgins giving birth. They say my father rose from dark depths, handsome and brooding. My mother broke the dam of his melancholy and brought him laughter and joy for the first time. I can't attest to the veracity of such tales; I'm only a child.

Mother takes to the streets at night, but when she walks beneath streetlights, those who see her are charmed into deep dreamy sleeps. In the morning, women wake with desire and men with erections, the population in the village doubles, even the old and infirmed give birth. Old men die of heart attacks, old women in childbirth. Orphanages fill with mouths they struggle to feed.

The constabulary sends a letter pleading with her to avoid the lights of night and to keep herself covered at all times.

That night, she strips and paints herself in green and autumnal colours, takes my hand and walks naked into the woods. Deer follow in her wake, birds fluff their feathers and sing at her approach, trees sway and leaves shimmer without wind. The moon lights a path before her. A parliament of owls, white and snowy, descend from stars, swoop her up and take Mother into the sky.

Alone and motherless, a murder of crows leads me home.

#

Alpheus Williams lives and writes in a tiny village tucked away along the coast of NSW, Australia. He spends a lot of time trying to explore and understand the unseen beauty of things.

Spacious Skies

by Emily Livingstone

The first giant squid to rise out of the water came out of the Atlantic, just off the coast of Maine. It propelled itself into the air, dripping warm saltwater on all below it, and it continued to swim, moving as easily through the sky as it had the water.

People marveled, staring upward, holding their smartphones up to document its trespass. News quickly spread, and as it did, more squid rose from the depths into the sky, basking in the sun, careening through clouds, looking down on the land dwellers with their alien fish eyes. Jellyfish soon followed, some smaller than teacups, some bigger than houses.

The sky was full of cephalopods, and inevitably, they had to eat. In Gloucester, Massachusetts, a giant squid reached a tentacle down and snatched up a woman walking right down Main Street. People screamed as the tentacles pulled her quickly to that hard beak. Then, most of them looked away.

The creatures could be killed, but not easily. Many were huge, and if they died over a populated area, they could crush hundreds of people. Some people shot at them anyway, unable to do nothing.

People tried to stay in their houses. When they went out, they sprinted to their cars. They watched the skies for shadows that were not clouds.

Storms were a wonder. The squid, especially, dove and played and spun their tentacles with obvious joy in the mixture of their old environment and their new one.

Scientists wondered how they managed it, these creatures who should be living at the bottom of the sea, in the cold and the dark. The prevailing theory was that the they'd adapted to warmer and warmer water, until the cold, and even the water itself, were no longer necessary. They were some of the sea's oldest inhabitants with a long time to change. Other sea life was nearly gone. Fish were found only in tanks. So these behemoths had surfaced to find other prey.

It was a nightmare. When the jellyfish ate people, the red flesh of their bodies showed up in the transparent stomachs, hovering like bad weather over their loved ones down below.

People didn't think it could get much worse. But then, the waters started rising rapidly. It was growing warmer and wetter. It rained without cease. The cephalopods swam in and out of the water as houses sank below the rising blue-gray tide. The government tried to build boats, to evacuate people to the mountains. All of it was too slow. The rich got out fast and left the poor behind. Those with boats struggled to add spikes to them to ward off seeking tentacles. It was a flood with no rainbow, filled with monsters.

People cowered, seasick, in the holds of ships. The beasts came and went in the sky and water. There was hardly any land anymore, and what there was, wasn't safe. Air travel was impossible. People were cut off from those they'd known. It was said that the waters hadn't reached everywhere, that the skies were clear over some places, and they went there on their pin-cushion boats, fleeing south, west, east, to places too hot for some of the creatures, where, by some miracle, they were not preying on the humans.

In some places, these travelers were welcomed. Their boats were given moorings. They were brought ashore and fed, cleaned, housed, comforted.

In some places, they took only the children, and left the adults marooned in the water, in a terrible limbo, waiting for unlikely salvation.

In some places, they promised mercy while delivering worse pain. They kept refugees in cells. People were sick, starving, and abused. They did not speak the language. They did not see the sky. They did not know if the cephalopods had come or gone. They wished for freedom. They wished for their families. They wished for safety. They wished for death. Sometimes, one of these wishes came true. Sometimes, a few.

#

Emily Livingstone is a writer, teacher, and mom living in New England and writing strange stories in the dark when the kids are asleep. Her work has been published in *The Molotov Cocktail*, *Necessary Fiction*, *Jellyfish Review*, *Atticus Review*, and others, and has been nominated for the Pushcart Prize and Best Small Fictions.

The Solemn Sequoia

by Alex Schweich

The storms it weathered. Standing tall and strong in silent solidarity with its sisters, tinted reddish-brown from ceaselessly bearing witness to the setting sun. Reinforcing its foundations layer by layer over hundreds of years, the ramparts sheltered its vulnerable veins from the barrage of heat, cold, rain, snow. Stretching towards the heavens, the lattice of branches, each as wide as a man is tall, rustled by the whistling wind. An occasional creak or moan, some solemn secret whispered in a language known only to the forest. Steadfast, resolute, a monument driven into the granitic soil of the Sierra Nevada range.

Or so it once was. The branches now were dry, parched, withering despite their hefty size. A flock of birds ceased their singing, disrupted by an indiscernible tremor coursing through the gnarled limbs. Leaves released their delicate hold, slowly fluttering to the ground. At times, the aged Sequoia seemed to sway, succumbing to a spell of vertigo reserved only for creatures who could think and speak. The vibrant hum of the natural world was proof of that consciousness, an esoteric awareness that linked its being to the subtle breath of the planet. The Sequoia could flourish or wilt, shed a teardrop of sticky sap or lift its branches into the curve of a smile. The Sequoia could speak in these ways, but no one bothered to listen, so the wizened tree appeared to them silent.

An airy melody floated up on the breeze. It came from a boy waltzing far below through the undergrowth, a lighthearted hum that resonated in the Sequoia's bones. Something that captured the visual awe—that pastel blend of luscious colors—with the sounds of seclusion and peace, those ephemeral moments when a bird sang or a footstep crunched on a fallen leaf—the kinds of melodies usually found only in the heart of this range-bound woodland. The gentle murmur was a beautiful thing to behold, but the boy kept it to himself under the volume of a whisper. Little did he know that a lonely tree was listening, wishing that its own refrain could be heard in turn.

The evening was growing tired, the sun slipping past the peaks on the horizon. Close behind the boy followed a father, a mother, and their daughter. With their arrival in the clearing, the boy stopped singing, much to the Sequoia's dismay. It was more than that; the others brought a clamor, a strangled cacophony of garbled inflections mixed with aimless movements and meaningless chatter. There was no grace in the way they talked, filling a void with dialogue just so there wouldn't be silence. The Sequoia longed to show them the beauty of a single moment of serenity, at least before its time was done. Something wondrous could be found in the stillness of its song.

After setting up their own shelter in the middle of the clearing, the parents pitched a tent for the children, searching for a protective awning that could guard them from the chill of the incoming twilight air. They found such solace under a thick, foliaged arm extending from the massive trunk of the Sequoia, fingers dressed in leaves reaching towards a distant companion. The wiry limbs of the ancient tree groaned an almost harmonious tune—yet haunting, as if to scream, "Get away," in a language foreign to the family. Its leaves rustled violently, begging for just a few feet to the left, but the outburst was disregarded.

After settling into his sleeping bag below the tree's fearful gaze, the boy began humming quietly once more. The Sequoia tried to squeeze out whatever moisture it had left—just enough for a single precious drop to slide down its face.

*

The night was bare and devoid of sound, save for a creaking like that of a rusted hinge and a distant melody whispered far below. A yawning and moaning, the strain of supporting a burden three thousand years old. The sorrowful Sequoia mourned the hazy hum of the boy's musical arrangement seeping through the porous fabric of the tent, wafting upwards until it brushed the edge of the canopy, waiting to evaporate.

It almost seemed like the boy's song could mend the frail limbs, but the weight of time's end was too much to bear. As the dry rot severed the last few fibers clinging to its trunk, the exhausted branch plummeted with a merciless whoosh and a deafening crash, followed by absolute silence that even the parents' agonized screams couldn't break.

#

Alex Schweich is a young author living in Southern California. You may think he loves the year-round perfect weather, but in truth, he yearns for torrential rain and snow. Fortunately, he'll get just that when he goes to study at Oxford this fall.

Agave Armageddon

by Wiebo Grobler

"Change your ways darlin', change your ways." The music crackles over the AM and drifts across the sand in a ghostly whisper.

The horizon stretches out like a taut wire in the distance as heat waves dance to the beat of cicada song.

"I fucking hate the desert. Time stands still in this place." Mark pulls hard on his cigarette, trying to smoke the taste of last night's tequila out of his mouth.

Tiny black beetles scamper across the red dirt, following a highway of small crisscross tracks.

Gary straightens and stretches his back, sweat trickling down the side of his neck. High above, an airliner makes its way across the sky, white contrails marking its progress against a backdrop of blue. Gary holds out his hand and Mark pulls him from the hole.

"Right, let's finish this." Mark flicks his cigarette into the pit.

Gary drops his shovel and they walk back to the car. Mark opens the trunk and they maneuver a large suitcase from the rear. They carry the case between them and then dump it into the hole. Their passage from the car is marked by small, wet crimson dots on the hot sand which fold up into tiny origami flowers made from blood and dust as it dries.

Mark pulls the old .38 from behind his back and fires three rounds into the suitcase.

Gary sneers. "What's that for?"

Mark puts the gun away. "Makin' me come out to the desert, that's what."

It is dusk by the time they finish covering the hole. The sun is a burnt mandarin, setting in the distance.

The radio has fallen silent. They throw their shovels into the trunk and climb into the car. Gary tries to start the Oldsmobile, but the fuel pump only ticks when he turns the ignition.

Gary smacks the steering wheel. "Goddamn battery!"

"One of us will have to walk back."

"I'll go. You know I can't stand waitin'." Gary gets out and pops the trunk. He grabs an aluminium torch. "I'll see you in a few hours. Stay by the car."

Mark nods and climbs into the driver's seat. He throws the pistol in the glove compartment, lowers his seat as far as it will go, sighs and closes his eyes.

*

Mark's eyes snap open. He wipes his hand across his face and checks the radium glow on his watch. He'd been asleep for forty minutes. Something woke him. The bark of a coyotes, chirp of crickets and hoot of owls, none of these he could hear. It was far too quiet.

He rolls down his window and strikes a match, squinting at the sudden flare. He lights a cigarette and flicks the match out the window.

There is movement out there, he can hear it.

Mark sticks his head out the window. "Gary?"

He recoils as something strikes him across the face. He

158

frantically rolls up his window and fumbles inside the glove compartment for his pistol.

The right side of his body throbs and burns. He gingerly runs his fingers across his face and flinches. Small needles riddle his flesh.

"What the fuck?" he moans and cuts his tongue.

Hissing in pain, he slowly starts to pull them out. They look like cactus thorns. Some prick had thrown him with a cactus. He switches on the car headlights. They glow to life briefly, illuminating the outside in a phosphorous yellow before dimming back into darkness. There are cacti everywhere. He is certain there weren't any this close by before.

Mark's skin is changing color, becoming lumpy and bruised. He opens the car door and stumbles out.

"Gary!"

There is movement all around him now, he can hear it, a scrape and shuffle. Mark runs, firing his pistol into the darkness. The report, like thunder, rolls across the desert.

Each shot brings a flare of bright light. Green limbs absorb the bullets without a flinch. They keep coming, moving on an exposed root system like tendrils of white varicose veins, roving across the ground, searching.

Mark stumbles and falls over something soft and wet. It is Gary—or what is left of him. It looks like he's fallen into a meat grinder.

The right side of Mark's body begins to stiffen and turn green. He screams as thorns tear through his skin from the inside out.

He brings his pistol up to his temple and pulls the trigger. There is an empty click. He can hear them. Voices inside his head.

Humanity's time has come.

An army of angry self-aware cacti—one with a pistol embedded in its limbs—turns towards the city lights shimmering in the distance like a neon mirage.

Above it all, Vegas Vic waves, welcoming the green apocalypse.

#

Wiebo Grobler is still trying to master walking upright. Fueled by a dwindling supply of O2, he walks the dream. Occasionally to wake up and write before the dream takes over again. To see more of his lucid work, join him on Twitter: @Wiebog or his website: wiebog.com.

Caddisman

by Michael Carter

There have always been three things we fear in the canyon cut by time and the ripples of the Gallatin River, and we have learned to survive each one.

The black bear: stand tall and stretch out your arms; yell; discharge your pepper spray; shoot to kill; fight back.

The grizzly: discharge your pepper spray; shoot to kill; lay flat on your stomach, place your hands behind your neck, and play dead. Pray.

The Caddisman: avoid eye contact; shoot to kill.

While I prepare to fish the canyon, I rehearse these rules in my head.

I strap cans of pepper spray to my wading belt. I place my Ruger into its chest holster. Finally, I pick my flies—golden stones, hoppers, lightning bugs, and Copper Johns. Most importantly, I load my fly box with Elk Hair Caddis flies, sizes twelve, fourteen, and sixteen.

I walk to the back acreage and make my way through the rye fields. My rod is in one hand, the other hangs low to brush the rye stalks. Their smooth silkiness makes me forget what Father Time has inscribed on my hands, and my face.

The wind gusts, tearing free fluff from the cottonwoods. It blows pollen from the evergreens. My eyes water.

As I near the trees, I see warning signs of what we fear. First, scat. It might be black bear dung, but perhaps another animal.

Next, where the field transforms to the vegetation near the river, gouges mark a pine tree. They are deep and wide enough to match grizzly claws. I pause and notice a bush stripped of most of its berries. Some remain. Perhaps the bear is satiated.

The temperature cools as I move through the bushes and descend off the cutbank ledge. Cobblestones embedded in a muddy mat welcome me. I step onto a glistening rock, wobble, but my felt soles secure my footing. Black leeches and mottled sculpins dart from the vibrations to deeper water.

I don't notice any hatches; only a single spruce moth flutters over the water. A hundred scenarios race through my mind, passed down like heirlooms and learned from a lifetime on the water. I might need a nymph rig, but I decide hopper-dropper.

My fly box open, I reach for a hopper. I change my mind. Upriver appears something I've seen only a few times before. Another sign. A cloud makes its way toward me, a ball of insects swarming, some of them dabbing the water. Trout explode in a frenzy below the ball, swallowing whole the pale insects that contact the surface.

They look like caddis. I tie on a size twelve Elk Hair Caddis, lay out my line, *ten o'clock, two o'clock,* and release my cast. My leader uncurls, and my fly lands in a crease. It floats naturally. I mend my line.

The cloud nears. The trout are still boiling below it, following under the surface as it moves downriver. I cast toward it, mend, nothing. I have only one more shot before it passes. The boil is right in front of me. I cast into it. Fish rise and splash around my fly, but there are no takers.

It passes without a strike. *This is why they call it fishing, not catching.*

My opportunity to hook one from the boil is gone, but there are still fish in the river. I sniff the crisp mountain air. I smile and think, *the worst day fishing beats the best day working.*

Movement at the corner of my vision breaks me from the solace of the moment. Peering through the undercarriage of the berry bushes, I make out two legs striding just beyond the river's edge.

"Who's there?" My words echo back to me off the canyon wall.

A manlike figure approaches the water's edge, near where I entered. He comes from behind while I face the river. I can feel his stare.

He gets closer, a stone toss away. His skin flutters.

I freeze. He comes within feet, his surface crawling with life. He's light tan, same as my elk-hair fly, but taking its hue from the thousands of caddis that coat his body.

He's standing behind me now, slightly elevated on the cutbank while I remain on the cobblestone below. The buzz of his living skin intensifies. *Should I run?*

Arms reach around me, and in front of my face I see hands. Insects flicker and undulate upon whatever being is underneath. As the arms constrict, I duck to the side.

The water splashes in front of me. He thrashes in the current like he's in pain. The trout rise again, their spotted heads and fins breaking the surface, framing the contours of a body. With their small, sawlike teeth—designed to crush the armor of beetles and hoppers—they tear into him. Red ribbons trickle down the river, stark against the cream of the floating caddis carcasses.

I pull out my Ruger and aim between where eyes might be. But then I hear something. *A cry, a plea?* The voice sounds familiar.

I toss my gun to the side. I lean toward the water.

A fleshy arm spotted with ruby pockmarks emerges with an open, welcoming palm.

We clasp hands. The remaining, clinging caddis crawl from his arm to mine. I feel the power of the river flow into my veins, and through me.

With all my strength, I pull. But his hand goes limp and slips away, disappearing under the foamy crests of the river.

The big sky becomes small as I'm engulfed in a blizzard of tan.

My skin tingles from the settling of countless tiny feet, and the tips of tented wings.

#

Michael Carter is a writer from the Western United States. He comes from an extended family of apple orchardists in Washington and homesteaders in Montana. He enjoys cast-iron cooking and wandering remote areas of the Rocky Mountains with his dog Hubbell, primarily along the banks of the Gallatin River. He's online at michaelcarter.ink and @mcmichaelcarter.

Sit, Stay, Play Dead

by Emma Miller

I've gotten out of worse than this.

Henny's breath is hot and rancid on my neck.

Once, like an idiot, I broke a crampon and fell 30 feet into an ice climb. But I kept calm, kept warm, and hiked out. Broken clavicle hurt like a mother, but was all healed up by spring.

Henny licks my frostbitten ear.

Once I got caught in a flash flood. Armed with only my quick wits and an overwhelming desire *to not fucking die,* I felt out high ground and made it home for dinner.

Henny sniffs the crotch of my down suit.

The trick is to stay calm. That's your best asset out here: your composure. And I have composure in spades. I'm the Blind Outdoorsman, for Christ's sake. Never let it hold me back. I have the speaking fees of an Obama and the Twitter following of a Hadid.

Henny whimpers.

I can't move. But I can't panic. So I count. *Two-point-eight million followers.*

My publicist says I could blow up on Instagram if I'd just apply myself. I point out the obvious challenge of photo platforms, but he brushes me off. *The dog*, he says. *They love pictures of the dog.*

Henny moans again, a quiet, keening whine. It's higher pitched than it was this morning. She's getting antsy, poor girl. I hear the steady hush of water nearby, so I don't think she's thirsty. But she's been pulling the supply sled on unforgiving terrain, and the dog food is sealed in a bear-proof bag.

It's nothing I can't handle.

What stings is that this is my own damn fault. I insisted on going solo. I promised to call when I made it to Anchorage. I said the crossing would take me a week, max. Luckily, this is day five. If I don't show up in two more, they'll send the cavalry. When I sleep (if I sleep), I dream of the sweet, sweet chop of helicopter blades. Just need two days.

Henny paces. *I know you're confused, girl. I am, too.* I don't know what happened. A parasite? A seizure? Another unfair kink in my genetics? What I do know is that one moment I was upright, the sun warm on my face, and then I was on my stomach in the snow. Every muscle mutinied. A stroke or just a stroke of fate—whatever it was, the effect has been unwavering. And the effect is that I can't move.

I can't turn my head to slow the tingling frostbite on my cheek. I can't lift my hand to reach the satellite phone trapped under my chest. And I can't click my tongue to reassure her.

She's been wandering in wider and wider circles—I can hear the scraping of the sled—but she always comes back. *I'm sorry, girl. I know you're cold. I know you're hungry.*

I can't panic. And so I keep counting. *Forty.* It's been 40 hours since I fell, judging by the beeps of my watch. Each *blip* is thunder to my noise-starved ears, so I doubt I've missed any.

The good news is I'm exerting zero energy, lying here. I've only pissed myself the one time. The down suit keeps me warm, but not sweating. All together, this will extend the dehydration window. That Boy Scout stuff about "three days without water" is crap: I've heard of people going as much as ten. So I'll be gross as all hell when they find me, but hey, alive's alive.

Ninety-five. It's fewer than 95 miles to my endpoint. In a world far from this one, a car could cover that distance in an hour and a half. Could really go for one of them right now. Lacking that, I meditate. I count. I keep calm. I have to.

Henny's footsteps crunch in the snow, punching new holes in the icy surface. It puts me on edge when I hear her leaving; it puts me on edge when I hear her come back. She's making that goddamn keen again.

A buddy of mine tangled with a bull shark a couple years back. Said his calf muscle sloughed off like silly putty. Teeth are as imprecise a tool as you can get.

Gotta stay calm.

I count. *Nine.* A working sled dog can eat up to 9 pounds of meat in a day—

No, not that one. Better choose another.

Four million USD. If things do go south, that's what I'm leaving my parents. The rest will go to the organization that paired me with Hen. Guide dog training, best in class. But that's only for when the worst happens, which won't be today. I mean, I always figured it'd be too soon and doing something stupid, but this isn't going to be it. This is easy peasy. All I have to do is lie here. Two more days, and then the cavalry.

When hikers die in the tundra, the wildlife goes for the soft bits first. Eyes, tongues, genitals, neck.

Nope. Can't panic. I count. *Fifty.* She is fifty paces away. No, forty. Is she getting closer, or further? The wind's picked up again and makes it hard to tell. Thirty paces. Christ, it's cold. And then—*zero.*

Henny nuzzles my shoulder, breath hot on my cold skin.

The fur around her mouth has frozen and melted and refrozen, leaving it sharp and solid, a matting of little needles.

Yes, Henny. Good Henny. I love you, Henny.

She pauses. Nuzzles again. Harder. The keening whine. It echoes across the emptiness around us, vibrates at the place where my spine meets my skull.

No, Henny. Gentle, Henny.

Just two days. Can't panic. Count. *Nine pounds.*

No, Henny.

But that's exactly what it is: no Henny. There is no Henny left here.

Her whiskers scratch my face—*no, Henny*—and my frostbitten cheek is ripped from the ground—*noHennynoHenny*—and then the stench of carrion dog breath and a burning hot as gasoline—*stay calm stay down stay STAY*—

#

Emma Miller is a writer and editor in New York City, where she writes facts by day and fiction by night. Her work has appeared in *The Molotov Cocktail, Daily Science Fiction, Apparition Literary Magazine, Flash Fiction Magazine*, and other outlets.

The Grove

by Aeryn Rudel

When I was a boy, the trees grew faster in the old grove behind our house. Faster than they should, faster than what you could call natural. They had a strange look to them, too, those trees. The patterns in the bark took on familiar shapes if you stared at them long enough, almost like faces.

The trees grew fast and took things from the ground, bits of furniture, an old tricycle, the skeletons of small animals. Once I saw the skull of a coyote sticking straight out of a branch ten feet off the ground. Grinning white teeth, eye sockets empty but still staring down on you like it was watching.

Daddy told us not to go into those woods or listen to the wind whistling through the leaves, rustling the branches like shaking, terrified voices. I didn't pay any heed to his warnings—too young, too curious. I would stand at the edge of the grove where the trees are still small and imagine the trees were talking to each other. Maybe they were.

My brother Johnny disappeared when I was ten and he twelve, and Daddy said the trees had taken him. I remember

Momma telling him to hush with that talk or he'd scare us children. We grieved, and things were quiet for a while.

Then Nancy, my little sister, disappeared six months later. When Momma went into town to arrange the funeral, to buy the empty box we would mourn over, she left me at home with Daddy. He was in a bad way, crying and cursing. I tried to calm him down, and I thought I did, but it wasn't calm. It was quiet resolve. He got an axe from the tool shed and went into the grove. I followed, begging him to stop and come back.

Daddy went deeper in, raving at the trees, hitting the big ones with the axe, making them bleed sap like black blood. I heard the wind rattling in the branches overhead, scraping and scratching. The trees were talking, and as I hurried after Daddy, they seemed to close in, the canopy of leaves eating the sky like a green shroud.

When I caught up to Daddy, he stood at the base of a big tree, feet planted, swinging the axe with all his strength. Bits of wood chipped and flew, and that old black sap splattered the nice white shirt Momma bought him for the funeral.

I tried to stop him, but he shoved me away. "Look at it, David," he said. "Look at the thing that ate your sister. Can't you see her face?"

I didn't understand that, but it scared me, and I begged him to quit and come back to the house. The rattling in the branches got louder, and it sounded angry. Those trees weren't talking now, they were screeching their hate down at us.

A branch broke off from one of the boughs, big and heavy, and it fell on Daddy, knocked him down and pinned him to the ground. I tried to push it off, but I wasn't strong enough. It lay on his stomach, and blood ran out of his mouth. He told me to run, to get Momma and enough kerosene to burn the grove.

I did run, all the way home, the trees scraping and scratching overhead. Sometimes it seemed the branches dipped against the wind, like they were gonna block my path. I pushed on until I reached the boundary of the grove and the grass beyond.

When Momma got home I was in tears, terrified and ranting. She grabbed hold of me and held me until I stopped shaking, until I could tell her what had happened. It was dark then, but she grabbed a flashlight and told me we'd find Daddy, right now. I told her about the kerosene, but she wouldn't get it. She said it was Daddy's sadness talking, making him do terrible things.

We ran into the forest and it had grown quiet, the wind nothing but a trickling gust. When we reached the place where the branch had fallen, Daddy was gone. Momma called out for him, running around the spot where I'd left him, her voice echoing off the trunks. I stayed put, remembering what Daddy had said about the tree that had eaten Nancy. I looked up and caught a flash of white. Then I screamed.

Daddy was half inside the tree, twenty feet off the ground. His head and arms dangled, and the rest of his body had been swallowed by the bark, like it had grown up around him, absorbing him into the heartwood. He was still alive, looking down on me, eyes bulging from their sockets, blood dripping from his mouth. I knew that tree was eating him, growing as it sucked the flesh and blood from his body, just like that coyote I'd seen.

Momma found me soon after, grabbed me, and ran. I don't know if she saw what I saw, but she never spoke about that day, not even on her deathbed last year.

We moved away a month later, and I haven't been back in twenty-five years. I think about the trees often. Do they still take things from the ground to carry off and eat? If I went back to the edge of the grove and listened, would I hear the trees talking with the voices of those they'd taken? Would I hear my father's voice? My brother's? My sister's? Would I want to follow?

\#

Aeryn Rudel is a writer from Seattle, Washington. He is the author of the *Acts of War* novels published by Privateer Press, and his short fiction has appeared in *The Arcanist*, *Factor Four Magazine*, and *Pseudopod*, among others. He occasionally offers dubious advice on writing and rejection (mostly rejection) at www.rejectomancy.com or Twitter @Aeryn_Rudel.

The Molotov Cocktail

www.themolotovcocktail.com

The Molotov Cocktail

Made in the USA
Coppell, TX
11 August 2022